Last Resort

~ The Grayton's ~
Cassey & Luke
© 2014 Jill Sanders

D0111665

Follow Jill online at:
Jill@JillSanders.com
http://JillSanders.com
Jill on Twitter
Jill on Facebook
Sign up for Jill's Newsletter

Dedication

To my wonderful husband and kids,
who listen to me talk about my book friends
way too much.

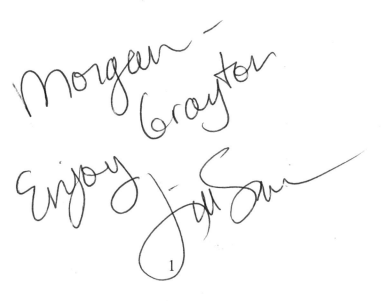

1

Summary

Cassey's life is crazy enough. The last thing she needs is some cocky rich boy trying to destroy her business. Normally immune to these vultures, she finds this brazen hottie especially difficult to refuse.

Out to close the deal of a lifetime, Luke won't take no for an answer, and the intoxicating beauty standing in his way isn't going to go down easily. He'll need more than business savvy to close this deal.

Table of Contents

Jill Sanders

Last Resort

by
Jill Sanders

Prologue

She was running for her life. Knowing what she would see if she looked back, she kept her eyes trained forward. She tried to avoid roots or limbs that might trip her up, taking each step as carefully as she could at this speed. Her mind flashed to images of what she'd witnessed minutes before, yet she was oddly clear about what she needed to do for a seven-year-old.

Branches scraped her legs and arms as she ran, and her breath hitched with every step she took. Her ears were straining to hear if she was being chased, but she couldn't hear anything beyond her breathing and her loud heartbeat.

When she couldn't run any longer, she ducked behind a large tree and squatted until she was in a tight ball. She tried to slow her breathing down so she could listen, but it took forever to get her breath under control. She didn't hear the footsteps until a shadow fell a few feet from her.

Wrapping her arms around her knees, she waited for what she knew was coming. She was sure she knew what the outcome of the night would be, so nothing could have prepared her for what happened next.

"Are you all right?" a soft voice asked next to

her.

Her head jerked up. Her long, dark, stringy hair got in her face, so she shoved the strands away with her dirty hands.

She looked up and noticed the angel who stood over her. Everything about the woman was aglow; even the woman's clothes shined in the evening light. Her long blonde hair looked soft, softer than anything Cassandra had ever seen. The woman's hands were stretched out to her, and she could see gold rings on almost every finger.

"Here now, no one is going to hurt you anymore. Come with me, Cassandra. I'll keep you safe." The woman's soft voice almost mesmerized her.

Slipping her little, dirty hand in the woman's larger one, she sighed as she felt her soft, warm skin next to hers. She'd never experienced anything so soft in her life.

"How?" she whispered, looking around just in case. "How do you know my name?"

The woman shook her head. "I'll tell you in the car. Come on, we have to move; they're on their way here now."

Cassandra could hear them now. The sound was almost deafening to her tiny ears as her heart rate spiked. She bolted from her hiding spot and ran beside the woman.

The road, which she'd been told never to go

near, was only a few feet from them, yet the limbs were thicker here and they had to fight their way through it. The woman's dress ripped as thorns pulled at it. Cassandra's legs and arms bled as deep scratches appeared on her skin.

Finally, they hit the clearing and the woman pulled open a car door.

"Quick, get in." She rushed around to the driver's door and jumped in.

Cassandra sat in the large front seat, her legs tucked up to her chest, her eyes glued to the trees, waiting, watching.

As they sped off, she sighed and her eyes slid closed for just a moment as she let her guard down. Then she opened them and looked at the woman.

"Who are you? How do you know my name?"

The woman smiled at her and glanced in the rearview mirror.

"My name is Lilly. I'm your caseworker."

Cassandra's eyes were glued to her. "What is that?"

Lilly chuckled. "It's like a guardian angel." She smiled and put her hand over Cassandra's hair. Cassandra flinched away, not knowing what the gesture meant. She'd never been touched so softly before.

"What's a guardian angel?" she asked, sliding

towards the door a little more.

"Someone who makes sure that you will never be hurt again."

"How are you going to do that?" Cassandra got up on her knees and looked out the back window of the car, making sure they weren't being followed.

"By taking you somewhere where they can't find you. I know this place"—she smiled, looking down at her—"where kids like you can be safe."

Cassandra doubted there was a place like that. Looking out the window of the car as it traveled quickly down the dark road, she thought that there wasn't anyone out there like her. Especially not someone who had gone through what she had. She knew why she had suffered, why she'd been forced to do things she didn't want to—she was the devil's child. Or so her father and stepmother had told her for as long as she could remember.

Her stepmother, Kimberly, had entered her life when she was two. She didn't remember much from before that, but her father had told her that her mother, whom he described as an angel, had died giving birth to her. She had hoped that Kimberly's arrival would save her from the hell she was living—never leaving a ten-by-ten-foot cell—but she quickly learned that wouldn't be the case. This became very clear when Kimberly beat her that first week for stealing a piece of her bread.

As the car drove down the dark highway,

Cassandra fell asleep, her little body tense even in sleep. She woke when they came to a stop.

"Sorry, I have to stop for gas. Would you like something to eat?" Lilly asked gently.

"Yes!" she thought. But she knew better than to answer an adult's question. Looking down at her hands, she shook her head.

"Well, I'm starving." Lilly's voice was so calm, it almost made Cassandra believe she could trust her. "You stay put. Promise me?"

Cassandra glanced at the woman. Her smile was so bright. Her blue eyes looked so kind. If ever there was an angel, Cassandra believed it was her caseworker, Lilly. Nodding her head, she looked back down at her dirty hands.

Lilly got out of the car, shutting the door gently behind her.

Cassandra didn't watch as she pumped gas; she kept her eyes and head down like she'd been taught. But when Lilly walked towards the little gas station, she picked her eyes up and glanced towards the building. After she saw Lilly walk through the doors, she looked around. This was a new place. It wasn't the gas station her father had stopped at. This was someplace she'd never been before. Her eyes got wide as she looked at the bright lights. There were large machines sitting right outside the doors.

Cassandra couldn't read well, so she didn't

know what the red and white words said. She'd learned her colors from a book she'd had when she was four. Red was spelled R-E-D. She knew all the colors and often would close her eyes and remember every page of the small cloth book that her stepmother had burned one day when she'd been looking at it instead of sleeping.

When she saw Lilly walking back, she quickly ducked her head back down, looking at her dirty fingers. Then she noticed the dirt on the carpet of the car from her shoes. Jumping down, she quickly picked up the larger pieces and shoved them into her mouth and tried to swallow them.

"Here now," Lilly said, getting into the car. "What are you doing?"

"Nothing." She sat back up and prayed that the woman didn't see the dirt she wasn't quick enough to get.

"What do you have in your mouth?" Lilly asked.

"Nothing," Cassandra said again, looking out the window. Tears were streaming down her face.

"Cassandra, look at me, please." The "please" broke through her defenses, and she looked over at the woman.

"I'm not going to hurt you. No one is going to hurt you again. I promise. Now tell me what you have in your mouth, please."

"Dirt," she blurted out. "I'm sorry. I got dirt in

your pretty car. I didn't..." She stopped talking and jumped away when Lilly reached over and touched her hand gently.

"Cassandra, look down here." She pointed to her side of the car. Dirt was all over the floor, even on her clothes. "I'm dirtier than you are, I think." She smiled at her and something shifted in Cassandra's heart.

"You..." She took a deep breath. "You aren't mad at me?"

Lilly shook her head. "No, honey. Now open your door and spit the dirt out. It must taste gross."

Cassandra did as she was asked. She'd learned long ago to always do what grownups told her to.

"Now, I bet this will taste a great deal better." She pulled a white bag between them. "I know it's not good to give children soda, but I think this one time we can make an exception." She pulled out a can that looked just like the machine she'd been looking at earlier.

"What is it?" Cassandra asked and then quickly tucked herself into a ball. She knew better than to ask questions. She must be tired to let her guard slip so much.

"It's okay, honey. You can ask all the questions you want. It's called a Coke. Would you like to try it?"

Cassandra nodded.

"I have a turkey sandwich and some potato chips here. I bought enough for you, just in case you got hungry. We still have a long way to drive before morning."

Cassandra looked at the sandwich. It was wrapped in a bag, and the chips were her favorite kind. She'd snuck one from Kimberly's large bag once and had gotten a whooping, but it had been worth it.

Lilly took out another sandwich and a bag of potato chips and started eating. Cassandra watched her for a few minutes, and then slowly reached over for the food. She wasn't starved. Her father had seen to it that she'd looked plenty healthy when the police showed up, but she was given only what she needed.

"Kids don't need to eat much. After all, all you do is sleep and poop," her father had told her over and over. She always thought there was something wrong with her because she wanted to go outside and play—to run in the dirt road, to jump off the tire hill that was in their front yard, or to just lay in the grass and watch the clouds go by.

She slowly opened the bag and took a bite of the sandwich. It was good. So good, she quickly ate every crumb. When Lilly opened the bag of chips for her, she ate every last one of those. Then she heard a noise she hadn't heard before and jumped.

"Would you like to try this?" Lilly held out the

Coke can. Cassandra nodded and took the soda. She took a sip and her eyes slid closed. The bubbles ticked her nose and made her throat feel funny. She looked over at Lilly. Lilly had a smile on her face. "It's good, huh?"

Lilly opened her own soda and drank from it. "Oh!" Lilly said, making Cassandra jump, spilling a little Coke on her clothes.

"I'm sorry." She started frantically wiping the dark liquid off her dirty clothes.

"Honey, it's okay. Don't worry about it." Lilly smiled at her. "I'm sorry for scaring you. I was just going to give you this." She pulled out a package from the white bag. "They're cupcakes."

There were two circles in a clear package. Cassandra had never seen anything like it. They had white swirly lines across them. Reaching over, Cassandra took them from Lilly's waiting hands.

"Thank you," Cassandra said and sat them on her lap before taking another drink from her soda.

"Well, aren't you going to eat them?" Lilly asked.

"They're awful pretty," Cassandra said.

Lilly laughed. "Yes, I suppose they are. Here, let me help you open the package."

Lilly opened the bag and handed one circle to her. When Cassandra bit into it, the richness sank into every pore of her little body. She felt goose bumps rise on her arms and legs. The little hairs on her entire body stood straight up.

"What is this?" Cassandra asked, a smile on her face for the first time.

"Chocolate," Lilly said, smiling back.

The rest of the car trip, Cassandra looked out the dark window and thought about chocolate. How could she get more? Where would she get more? Was it something everyone had?

Her little mind finally ran out of questions, and she rested her head against the car door again. She woke when the car stopped suddenly. This time, the sun was just rising.

"Here we are," Lilly said in a cheerful voice. "Your new home."

The place was huge. Cassandra looked out the front window and instantly was afraid. It had three stories and was cleaner than anything she'd ever imagined.

"There are four other kids around your age living here now, but others come and go. You'll enjoy it here." Lilly got out of the car after honking the horn several times. She walked around and opened Cassandra's door, smiling the entire time.

Cassandra shrunk herself back into the car seat, holding the empty cupcake package tightly to her chest. She shook her head, no.

"I don't wanna stay here."

Lilly knelt down beside her. "It's okay, honey. No one is going to hurt you here. I promise you."

Shaking her head again, she watched as three boys her age came running out the front door. Their clothes were clean and they had new shoes on their feet. Two had dark hair, one with blue eyes and one with dark brown eyes. The last boy had blond hair like Lilly.

Cassandra didn't know much about boys, but she knew they looked tough, and she didn't want to deal with them. She shook her head from side to side, faster.

"Look, here comes Marissa. She's your age and just arrived here last month."

Cassandra looked over just in time to see a girl around her age walk out the front door. She had a small kitty in her hands and was wearing a white dress and sandals. Her blonde hair was pulled back in short braids.

Cassandra looked at Lilly. "I know they have some chocolate in there and if you don't like it here, you can come home with me. Okay?"

Finally, Cassandra nodded and got out of the car, holding onto Lilly's hand as they walked up the front steps under the watchful eye of the four kids and four adults.

Cassandra didn't pay much attention to the kids since she knew the adults were the ones in charge. There were two women and an older man who looked frail. She knew she could outrun him if she had to. One of the women looked strong and capable; the other looked overweight and older. Cassandra knew that didn't mean she couldn't run fast since Kimberly had been pudgy and fast.

"Hi, everyone, this is Cassey." Lilly looked down and winked at her. Cassandra liked the shorter name; she'd always thought her name was too long and too big for her.

"Hi, Cassey," everyone said together.

"Cassey," Lilly said, smiling down at her, "this is Mr. and Mrs. Grayton. They own this house. And these are their daughters, Julie and Karen. Julie teaches school and will be responsible for you."

"Hello," she said under her breath.

"Hi," Julie said, kneeling down to her. Her hands were tan and she wore a faded pair of jeans and a button-up shirt with flowers on it. Her short brown hair was curly and looked soft like Lilly's. Her brown eyes looked rich and warm like the rest of her. "I've made some pancakes for breakfast. Would you like to come in and have some?"

Cassey looked up to Lilly and when Lilly nodded, she looked at Julie and said, "Yes, please."

Chapter One

Fifteen years later...

Cassey stood on the crowded boardwalk and looked at the slightly burned building. The windows were knocked out, the front door was boarded up, and a good chunk of the ceiling was falling in. It was perfect. She smiled one of her rare smiles and walked towards the doors. The keys were in her hands and her fingers shook as she slid the silver key home to unlock the large wooden door.

When it creaked open, she smiled again, knowing it belonged to her. Well, to her, her family, and the bank. She walked in slowly, keeping the doors open so the light from the boardwalk sifted in. Flipping on the lights, she noticed that tables and chairs were piled up against the back wall. Most of the old mirrors along the walls were broken, thanks, no doubt, to kids breaking in and tossing stones at them. But it wasn't such a great loss; she'd planned on taking them down anyway. The black ceiling and walls would be painted a lighter color since the place would no longer serve as a grunge dance club.

As she looked around the large room, her mind whirled with ideas, just as it had since she'd first seen the place almost eight years ago. Back then, her aunt, Julie's sister, had been running the dingy grunge club.

Cassey had spent years walking up and down the beach outside and knew the wonders the mile-long boardwalk held. Even though it was centered on the beach in one of the smallest towns along Florida's Gulf Coast, tourism had always been booming here. This was the *it* place to be. With it's small-town charm and quaint shops.

Most of those little shops were housed in one long building. They'd recently been painted a light yellow with tall white columns. Some units had upper floors, which usually housed apartments or offices. The little details of each section were unique, showing off the character of each business.

The businesses provided everything one might desire on a summer vacation. There were shops that sold sundresses and swimwear which sat alongside ice cream parlors and specialty shops.

There was a fun-plex of sorts at the other end of the docks that was almost always packed with kids, even during the off-season. She and her brothers had spent many hours and all of their allowance there during their school years. The only thing the boardwalk was missing was entertainment for adults. Cassey planned on providing it.

Smiling, she looked around the large room. There was a long mahogany bar against the left wall and a stage area in the back right corner that she planned on using. The tables and chairs that had been left there could even be cleaned up and used again.

The old building, which sat separate from the others, had been in the Grayton family for generations, and since waterfront property in the growing resort town of Surf Breeze was highly sought after, it needed to stay that way. Ever since her Aunt Karen's death two years ago, the family had been receiving offers for the old building.

It wasn't until Cassey's last birthday that she had made the decision to follow her dreams and take a chance. She'd worked at the local restaurant in Spring Haven since she was sixteen. Being a waitress had given her the experience she needed to open her own place. But her dream wasn't only about food. She smiled as she looked around. No, she had a few other plans for this place.

She took her time walking through the large

rooms. The large kitchen in the back would need new appliances, but other than that, it could be up and running with minimal work besides a good cleaning, some paint, and TLC.

The two customer bathrooms were standard and only needed cleaning and supplies. She walked back out to the main room and noticed the mirrored office hovering over the back corner. She knew she would be spending time there and decided to walk up and take stock of the shape it was in.

When she climbed the narrow stairway, she could smell burnt carpet. Walking into the office, she frowned. Here the fire had done the most damage. She could actually see through the roof and the water damage to the floor was pretty bad.

Turning down a long hallway, she walked towards what would be her home. She knew the apartment was furnished, but was afraid of what was in there. Using her other keys, she opened the heavy door and took another narrow hallway to her new apartment. The door to the small place was painted bright teal. She liked the color and smiled slightly, knowing she would keep it.

When she walked into the one-bedroom place, she was shocked. It was gorgeous. She'd never been back here; when they had visited eight years ago, they had stayed in the front building. Her Aunt Karen had lived here and had run the club since the early eighties. She had been the wild child, though she had always been accepted in the family.

Where Julie had been soft-spoken and very modest in her appearance, Karen had been her complete opposite. Even though their faces matched perfectly, the twins had chosen completely different attitudes and lifestyles.

She walked into the apartment and noticed the flowered colonial furniture. Karen's clothing style had always been dark, but her apartment reflected a more feminine side.

The tan tile floors needed a good cleaning, some of the furniture as well, but it was better than she had expected. Walking through it, she noticed the out-of-date appliances in the small kitchen. She knew her budget wouldn't allow for new ones just yet, but maybe she could find some used ones that were in better condition.

Walking to the back, she noticed the bathroom needed some work as well. When she walked into the bedroom, she gasped and rushed to the sliding doors. Outside, a small rooftop patio garden area was in full bloom. It hadn't been tended in the last two years since no one had lived there, but still the flowers and trees were beautiful. She made a mental note to buy some shears to trim back the bushes that had grown wild. An iron table and chairs sat in the middle of the stone pathway. On either side of the back-alley garden were low brick walls which helped kept the secret patio hidden. It was a small slice of heaven in the middle of grunge. She loved it. She could imagine herself spending most of her free time here, reading, working on her laptop, or just soaking up some sun.

Walking back in, she noticed the bedroom for the first time. A large four-poster bed sat in the middle of the room. Old white lace hung off the tall posts, giving a canopy look to the bed.

She tested the mattress; it was soft and would be comfortable enough. Lying back on it, she closed her eyes for a moment. She could do this. She was only twenty-two, but the business classes she'd taken while waiting tables would serve her well.

Her business plan had impressed the bank enough that they had given her a loan to fix the place up without batting an eye. Now all she had to do was get her hands a little dirty and get started.

Her brothers were going to be there first thing tomorrow morning, but she just couldn't wait to get started. Heading back out to her car, she grabbed her bags and carried them in through the side gate and walked up the outer stone steps to her new apartment. Changing out of her clean clothes, she pulled on a pair of old jeans and an old T-shirt. Tying her long dark hair back with a bandana, she pulled out a box of cleaning supplies from her car and got to work downstairs. The office would have to wait for her brothers to arrive since it would have to be gutted and someone would have to climb up on the roof to patch the holes. No doubt,

Marcus would be the one to get up there and do the patching.

Marcus had always been fearless. When she first arrived at the Grayton place fifteen years ago, she'd never imagined having three brothers and a sister to grow up with. But the kids had bonded and had been inseparable, at least until Marissa had run away suddenly, shortly after her seventeenth birthday.

Cassey frowned as she started to clean, thinking about her sister. She missed her and wondered what had caused her to leave such a wonderful place. Whatever it had been, she hadn't confided in her and that hurt worse than any beating she'd ever received from her real parents.

As she worked, she remembered the last night she'd seen Marissa. They had walked down to the lake and had gone swimming, something they had done since bonding the first summer they'd lived in the house on the hill with the Graytons.

"Do you believe in fate?" Marissa asked as she floated in the cool water, looking up at the dying light. Her long blonde hair floated around her tan face. She'd just turned seventeen three days earlier and they'd had a large party that weekend.

"Fate?" Cassey thought about it. "Sure, I guess so." She was floating, much like Marissa, but her dark hair was shorter and closer to her head.

25

"I'm destined to be like my mother," Marissa blurted out, causing Cassey to stand up and look down at her.

"Why would you say that?" she asked, frowning down at her sister. She'd heard the horror stories of Marissa's past. Her mother had had her when she was just sixteen. She'd been so into drugs, no one had thought that Marissa would survive the first week. But she had, and she'd lived long enough to suffer the wrath of a mother addicted to crack. At least until Lilly had swooped in, much like she had with Cassey, and rescued her.

Marissa had arrived at the Graytons less than a month before she had.

Marissa stood up in the water next to her, looking down at the round rocks along the shore. "I don't know. It's just some of the choices I've made in life." She shrugged her shoulders. "I see so much of her in me." Marissa looked up into Cassey's eyes. Cassey could see sadness there and something else in her eyes.

"What's wrong?" She moved closer to her.

Marissa looked up and shook her head. "Nothing. I guess I'm just being emotional." She smiled and then splashed water at her playfully. "I'll race you to the docks?"

Cassey took the challenge and lost, like always, and quickly forgot all about the conversation until the next morning when she'd gone in to wake

Marissa for school and found her bed empty with a note on the pillow. The note only said that she had to leave and nothing more.

Cassey blinked back to the now. She was losing the light, so she walked over and flipped on the overhead lights. A few bulbs were out, causing the room to be in shadows.

She'd wiped down the bar and cleared out the old bottles and trash from behind it. There were a few spots for small fridge units, and she knew the keg hold and lines would need some work. She planned on having a new soda machine installed.

Back in the kitchen, the pizza ovens were still in working order and she thought of adding flatbread pizzas to the menu along with fresh seafood items and some other favorites—burgers, steaks, and chicken dishes.

She worked until she was too tired to work anymore, but she was happy that the place was already looking better by then. As she cleaned, she added a dozen or more items she would have to buy or fix to her list. There was still so much to do before opening day, which she planned on being a little over a month from now.

She had applied for the liquor license when she'd signed up for her business license. It would take a few weeks for approval, but she had a few weeks to spare. The building inspectors were scheduled to stop by in three weeks, and there was so much to do before then.

27

Walking up the back stairs, she slowly made her way down the hallway to her new home. She plopped down on the bed, fully clothed, and was asleep before she could even remove her shoes.

"Is she dead?" a deep voice said above her.

"She looks dead. Poke her," another one said.

"I'm not going to poke her. Remember what happened the last time we woke her up?" the first voice said again.

"That's because you dumped a bucket of cold water on her head."

"It was your idea." There was a deep chuckle.

Cassey rolled over and covered her ears with her pillow as an argument ensued.

"Enough!" She sat up and looked into three gorgeous faces hovering above her. "How did you get in here?" She crossed her arms over her chest and frowned.

"You forgot to lock the front door." Marcus, the leader of the pack, spoke first. His smile was contagious as his dark hair fell over his eyes.

"You look like hell," Cole said. His blond hair was long and his blue eyes sparkled with humor.

"Shut up. Don't pester her," Roman said as he sat next to her. Roman had always been the sensitive one. His dark hair was neatly trimmed; his eyes were dark and had always been full of love. "Isn't it obvious? She's just tired. We should probably get to work and let her rest." He patted her hand.

Cassey sank back on her pillows and listened to her brothers start to argue again.

"Suits me," Marcus said, smiling. "More donuts for us." He turned to go.

"Donuts?" Cassey sat up again. "There wouldn't happen to be a raspberry-filled one in there?"

"Two," Marcus said, holding out a box from her favorite bakery, which was only a few doors down.

"I'm up…if you have—" She didn't even finish before Cole held out a tray of four cups of coffee.

"You three are saints," she said, moving slowly as she got out of bed. Every muscle in her body ached. Cole handed her a double-chocolate-chip Frappuccino and she took a sip and smiled. Then Marcus handed her a jelly-filled donut and her life was complete.

They sat out on the patio table as they ate their fatty breakfast and talked about the plans for the day. She knew her brothers would be there for her until the job was done. And they would work just as hard as she would, which made her love them even more.

By the end of three weeks, the place looked spotless. There had been a couple problems, but with help from her brothers and a few contractors they'd hired, everything had smoothed out.

The place had passed inspection with flying colors, and she now had her liquor license hanging behind the bar in a silver frame.

Opening day was less than two days away and still her brothers stuck by her side. She had most of her staff hired and was still training a few of them. The food and liquor had been delivered and Cole had helped out immensely in the kitchen, working with the staff she'd hired to make sure there were appetizing items on the menu that the customers would enjoy. They had even set up several tables and chairs out front for customers to sit at during the day. After all, Boardwalk Bar & Grill, or the BBnG as she liked to call it, would be open for lunch and dinner.

She stood back and watched the sign being lowered on to the front of the building. The letters of "Boardwalk" were in yellow, and "Bar & Grill" sat below it in white. The sign would glow at night, showing off the crisp letters.

She had smaller signs from some of her vendors posted in the new front windows. Awnings hung over the three large windows to shield customers from the hot sun as they dined out front in the gated areas. There were tall palm trees out front, which created shade, too.

Cole had suggested she hang planters on the large wood posts of the boardwalk, which closed in her patio area. Marcus had worked for three days to build the small boxes, which she filled with brightly colored tropical flowers.

The place looked wonderful, better than even she had envisioned. They'd painted the outside a dark teal blue with white around the windowsill and doorways, giving the old place a brand new look.

She watched as her brothers walked out the front doors. They looked good together. An image of watching them walk out of the Grayton house together that first time played in her mind. They looked the same, but different. Now they were all well over six foot. Their bodies and faces were different from one another, yet they were brothers in every sense. They would stick together through anything. Cassey smiled at them as they approached her.

"The place looks good," Marcus said, wrapping an arm around her shoulder. "Can you believe it? You're a business owner."

"I always thought that Roman would be the only entrepreneur," Cole said, throwing an arm around his brother and rubbing his shorter hair.

"Knock it off," Roman said, pushing Cole away.

"What needs to be done now?" Marcus asked, looking down at her. If she didn't think of them all as her brothers, she would swoon over the attention they gave her, but she'd never felt that pull towards any of them.

"Fliers." She smiled at them. "Opening day is two days away and we need to hit the beach and the streets." She had stacks of fliers she'd printed out on her new laser printer in her newly remodeled office the night before.

Cole groaned. "Aww, man. Really?"

"Hey, don't knock it. It's the best way to pick up girls. Remember that summer I spent working for Petro's?" Marcus smiled.

Roman laughed. "The summer you had twelve girlfriends?"

"The very same." Marcus smiled. "I'm game. But if you want to sit this one out, Cole," he said, grabbing his brother in a headlock, "maybe you don't like girls."

"Knock it off, you two," Cassey said under her breath. She was the peacemaker between her brothers. She'd broken up more fights and acts of roughhousing than she could count. Maybe that's why she'd never thought of them as anything but brothers.

For the next two days, Cassey stayed busy as her brothers handed out stack after stack of fliers.

When opening morning came around, she stood looking at her staff and her brothers in the main dining room.

"Is everyone ready for today?" Everyone shook their heads. "If there are any problems at all, don't hesitate to let me know. How's the kitchen?" She looked towards Sam, the head chef she'd hired two weeks ago. He was a middle-aged man who had a long line of impressive references.

"Great. Ready to get cooking." He smiled.

"Wendy, how's everything behind the bar?"

"Ready," her head bartender replied. "The last of the stock arrived yesterday, so we are up and ready. Can I just mention that I love that you took my advice on the blenders." She smiled a warm smile. Wendy had been invaluable and was quickly becoming one of Cassey's best friends. "I can't wait to whip up some mixed drinks."

Cassey nodded. "You've all been so wonderful." She looked down at her watch. "Now, how about we open those doors and see what happens. Stations everyone." She clapped her hands.

"What about us?" Marcus asked.

"Stand over there and look gorgeous…and flirt with all the single ladies." She smiled.

"Can do." He saluted her and then turned to his brothers. "Pure torture." They laughed as they walked over to the bar area and immediately started flirting with Wendy.

Cassey walked to the front doors, closed her eyes for just a moment, and took a deep breath.

A memory flashed in her mind. Her stepmother hovered over her as she screamed, "You will never amount to anything. You hear me girl? You are worthless."

Opening her eyes, she straightened her shoulders and flipped the lock on the doors. The sunlight hit her face and she smiled as she saw the long line of customers waiting outside.

Chapter Two

Two years later...

Cassey watched customers come and go. She knew what her financial books said and wondered why things weren't clicking. It had been two wonderful years, and she'd paid off half her loan in that short time, faster than she had imagined. But now something was wrong. Customers weren't coming as frequently. She had Sam change up the menus a little to reflect the changing styles. People always said how great the food and atmosphere were, but then she wouldn't see them again.

They had their regulars at the bar, and the weekends during the season were still good. However, in the last few weeks, she had seen a change and customers just weren't coming.

She stood out on the pier and frowned. There just weren't enough people walking by anymore. Even the shops next to her had suffered. She'd talked to the owners and all of them were baffled. Some buildings now sat empty with "for sale" signs in the front windows. Enough buildings sat empty that it was a great concern to the other business owners. Some of the business that had disappeared had been bought out, but there were still enough businesses and owners that were determined to stick it out, no matter what.

She'd been visited a few times by some of the larger resorts down the beach. Several had given her very appealing offers to sell out. But this was her family's place, not just hers, and she wasn't going to sell, period. She hadn't even mentioned the offers to the Graytons, knowing what they would say. The place had been in their family for generations and they were determined to keep it that way.

She leaned against the railing and watched as couples and children played on the beach. It was chilly today, with a cold wind coming in off the Gulf, so everyone was bundled up in jeans and light jackets. Fall was, in her opinion, the best season. The cool air rushed in off the ocean, cooling everything down.

This time of year always made her think of her family. Maybe because she'd always enjoyed taking the long drive across the Dolphin Bay Bridge back to Spring Haven and the old house on the hill that overlooked her small hometown. Even though the weather was usually nice, she could feel the changes and knew that even cooler weather was on its way.

Taking a deep breath, she went back to her office to work on a new business plan that would get the boardwalk and her bar and grill busy again. Walking into the main dining area, she looked around and noticed there were only four tables being served. For lunch, this was tragic.

Walking past the bar area and waving at Wendy, she went up the narrow stairs quickly. When she pushed open her office door, she was shocked to see a gorgeous man sitting behind her desk, fast asleep with his feet up. It took her a second to regain her composure as she looked at him.

His light brown hair was cut stylishly, with the top raised up and the sides shorter. Side burns ran to the middle of his ears. His long dark eyelashes lay on his checks. His jaw was square and one of the best features on his face. His lips. She couldn't take her eyes from them. They were full and looked like they would be fun to kiss.

He wore a blue, collared shirt, the top button open, with no tie. He wore a light tan leather bomber jacket and dark gray jeans. His black boots rested on the corner of her desk.

She'd never been one to deny herself physical pleasures with a good-looking man. Men were easy to come by when you ran one of the largest bar and grills along the beach. They were easy enough to discard as well. She was always quick in her affairs, never letting the relationships fester into something that got out of hand. Usually they only lasted a few weeks before she would get bored and move on.

Shaking herself from her thoughts and from watching the sexy man sleep in her chair, she closed the door loudly, and his eyes slid open slowly. They were dark brown and she could have sworn he was laughing at her.

He smiled at her, keeping his feet on her desk and his arms crossed over his chest.

"Oh, there you are," the man said in a rich voice. "I've been waiting for over an hour, you know." He finished as his eyes ran up and down her, much like she'd done to him.

"Who are you?" she asked, frowning. "And what are you doing in my office?" She walked over and pushed his boots off her desk. He smiled even more.

"Luke Callaway. I left you over a dozen messages." He stood and she realized how tall he was. Of course, at five-four, most men were taller than her. But he was impressive, probably an inch taller than Roman, the tallest of her brothers.

She quickly walked over and sat in her chair, making sure to straighten the papers he'd messed up. "I'm sure I would remember..." She dropped off as it dawned on her. Luke Callaway was the owner of Crystal Shores, one of the larger hotels in Emerald Beach, a few miles west of there. He and his minions had been the most annoying at trying to buy her out. Her spine tensed. "Yes, I remember now." She flipped open her laptop and logged in. "As I told all of your employees, I'm not interested in selling." She glanced up at him through her lashes. "Now, if you would be so kind as to leave my office."

He looked down at her and smiled as he took a seat on the leather couch that sat across from her desk. She tried not to sigh out loud as he leaned down and placed his elbows on his knees and looked at her.

"I understand. I just thought a friendly visit was in order." He looked at her and she felt heat spread down her body.

She turned to her computer. "I really don't have time for a chat at the moment."

He laughed at her.

"What?" She frowned and glared at him.

"I think we both know you have all the time in the world." He nodded to her almost empty dining room. "It's not like you're overrun with customers at the moment."

She stood and rested her hands on her desk as she glared at him. "You think this is funny? Everyone along the pier knows what you and the other resorts are doing to small business owners. I suppose we should have seen it coming, but now you march into my place and make yourself at home." She walked to the front of her desk, wishing she could grab the man up and force him out of her place. "Get out," she said under her breath. "I will say this for the last time. I am not selling my place, especially not to the likes of you." She walked to her door and opened it to wait until he stood and left. But he just leaned back on the couch and looked like he was going to make himself at home.

"You are a conundrum." His smile dropped away as he shook his head. "Like I said, I'm just here for a friendly visit."

She sighed and stood in the doorway as she crossed her arms over her chest. "We both know you are not here to *visit*," she said while grinding her back teeth. "So, would you mind telling me exactly why you are here?"

"Why don't you shut the door and have a seat, so I can explain." He motioned to her desk.

She took a moment to calm herself before shutting the door again. Instead of walking behind her desk, she leaned on the edge and crossed her arms, waiting for him to explain.

Luke waited until she settled herself on the edge

of her desk. Her silver eyes watched him carefully, as if she was waiting for him to go against his word.

He'd had a plan when he'd walked into the Boardwalk Bar and Grill—to get the owner, Cassey Grayton, to sell this place to him and his family.

His family had owned Crystal Shores, a large hotel in Emerald Beach, for several generations. Now, with his fresh college degree hanging behind his desk in his impressive top-floor office in a glass tower overlooking the Gulf of Mexico, he was ready to show his father what he could do. Acquiring this pier-front property was the first assignment. He leaned back and crossed his leg over his knee.

He hadn't planned on Cassey Grayton being so beautiful. When he'd opened his eyes and seen her standing over him, he'd first thought that he was dreaming. Her dark hair was tied up, but strands of it fell around her face in soft clumps. Her lips had drawn his eyes. They were full and looked like they were made to be kissed. They were the color of the petals of a delicate pink rose.

He looked up into those silver eyes and saw annoyance there. Smiling a little, he sighed, knowing he'd wasted enough time.

"Okay, just so we're clear, my intent is to get you to sell this place." She flinched and started moving towards the door. He was up quickly and grabbed her arm lightly.

"Wait, hear me out." He looked down at her. She was smaller than he'd first thought. The top of her head reached just below his shoulders.

"If you are going to stand in my office and lecture me about why it's a great idea to sell you my property, then there's the door." She nodded.

"No lecture." He smiled. "Only a friendly chat. I promise."

She looked at him for a few moments. His fingers were still wrapped around her arm lightly. She jerked her arm away and walked over to her desk and sat down. He followed her lead and sat back down on the couch.

"Why won't you sell?" he asked.

She closed her eyes and sighed. "Just like yours, this is a family business."

His eyebrows shot up. "I was led to believe that you were the sole owner."

"I am. However, this building and property have been in my family for generations. Much like your business has." She nodded to him. "I can't and won't sell this property." She leaned forward. "Now, why are you still sitting in my office?"

His smile was quick. "I like a woman who's quick to the point." He leaned forward, resting his elbows on his knees. "Go out with me tonight."

She blinked a few times and leaned back

quickly, as if she'd been slapped. Then a small crease formed between her eyebrows. "Why?"

"Why?" This time he frowned and then chuckled. "Because you're an attractive woman and fellow business owner. I'd like to spend an evening getting to know you better." What he wasn't telling her is that his father had told him not to return until the deed to her place was in hand. And that he got a strange flutter when she looked at him like she was doing now. Besides, he wanted to find out what was under those tight black pants and silky pink top.

"I'm sorry, Mr. Callaway. You'll just have to entertain yourself while in Surf Breeze." She turned to her laptop again and started punching keys. "Now, if you'll excuse me, I have work to do."

"Surely you can take a night off, at least once in a while," he said.

She looked up at him and waited.

His mind whirled, thinking of a way around the stubborn streak he'd just discovered in her. Then it clicked and he smiled. "Suit yourself. I'll show myself out." He got up and stood with his hand on the doorknob. "Let me know if you change your mind. I left my card there." He nodded to the edge of her desk. "My cell number is on the back." He turned and left.

Walking down the narrow stairs, he headed

straight for the bar. A pretty blonde was behind it, looking bored.

"Hi, what can I get you?" she said in a breathy voice as she leaned over the bar, showing off an impressive amount of cleavage. He was shocked that her flirting did little to arouse him and wondered why sad silver eyes popped into his head, instead.

It took almost two hours before Cassey walked down the back stairs. He'd sat at the bar the whole time, nursing a beer and asking Wendy, the bartender, every question he could think of about Cassey. When he noticed her walking down the stairs, his mind stopped for almost a minute. She'd changed from her casual black pants and shirt into something tight and sexy. Her heels gave her almost three inches and made her legs look... delicious. She'd done something with her hair and makeup that made her eyes look bigger and deeper. Her lips were painted a deep red, causing his eyes to zero in on them until she was standing a foot in front of him.

"What are you still doing here?" She looked annoyed. When he didn't answer right away, she crossed her arms over her chest, pushing her slight breasts together, and his mouth started watering. Why was he salivating over her small frame rather than the ample figure of the bartender? Then he looked up into those eyes and knew the answer. He wanted her. Wanted her like he hadn't wanted anyone else in a long time.

He leaned back against the bar and tried to smile, even though his heart was beating faster than if he'd just run a marathon.

"Well, I thought I'd stick around and see how you run the show." He nodded to the almost crowded room. The dining tables were turned over quickly, so the people lining up for a table didn't have to wait long. The dance floor was almost vacant, but so far, the DJ had only played prerecorded music. The sign out front said there was live music on Fridays and Saturdays. He wondered if the place really packed out on those nights.

"You're welcome to enjoy yourself, but I warn you." She leaned closer and he got a quick whiff of her perfume, causing his eyes to close momentarily in ecstasy. "If you interfere with any of my staff, or with me, I'll have Tyrone haul you out." She nodded to a dark man who looked like he'd just walked out of the ring at a WWW match.

He smiled at her and then shocked himself when he gently ran his fingertips down the outside of her arm. She jumped and scowled at him, causing him to smile even more. Her skin was feather soft and he knew without a doubt that he had to get his hands on it again.

She turned and walked away quickly. He watched as she mingled with customers, laughing and talking with each table. She had a way about her. He couldn't deny it; she was born for this. By the time she'd visited each table, she looked more relaxed than he'd seen her.

She approached the bar and asked for her usual. He smiled when Wendy handed her a Coke. He slid down the bar to stand next to her.

"Busy night." He watched her tense and wondered what it would take for her to relax around him.

"Not as busy as it used to be." She took another sip of her drink.

"Is it just me? Or do you dislike everyone that walks in here trying to buy your place?"

She sighed and looked at him, tilting her head. "I haven't decided yet."

He chuckled, and then felt the full force of how truly beautiful she was as she smiled.

Chapter Three

Cassey's heart skipped when Luke looked at her like that. She had wavered about approaching him in the first place. When she'd walked down the stairs and seen him resting against her bar, she'd wanted to run back upstairs and hide. The funny thing was, she didn't know why.

She'd dealt with all his employees, some of them very good-looking men, easily enough. But there was something unsettling about Luke's eyes and his smile. If she was honest with herself, she would admit that it was the instant attraction that had slammed into her gut when she'd seen him. But she wasn't at the point of being truly honest… yet.

"I'm not going to change my mind, you know." She took another sip of her Coke, wishing the cool bubbles would sooth the fire that was raging inside her.

"I have no doubt about that." He started running his fingertips over her arm, like he'd done before. She felt sparks everywhere he touched her and while part of her wanted to pull away again, it felt so good to be touched. Not since she'd broken it off with Mark a few weeks ago had someone shown this much interest in her.

In the back of her mind was the nagging feeling that he was trying to find her weakness so he could swoop in and buy this place from under her, that he was trying to use sex to soften her up. It would never work, so she had to wonder why he was trying so hard.

It was so hard to gauge his intentions. His chocolate eyes revealed little of what he was thinking.

"Then why are you sticking around?" she asked as she tried to push his fingers from her skin. Instead, he laced his hand with hers, holding her still.

"I think you know why," he said, just under his breath.

Shaking her head slightly, she realized she had been holding her breath. "No." It came out weaker than she'd intended.

Somehow, he'd moved closer to her, so that their knees and shoulders were touching now. She could smell his rich scent, which caused her insides to do a little flip. Even her legs felt weak now as he ran his other hand over her exposed knee. She'd crossed her legs, but now she realized how vulnerable it made her feel. Wishing she'd worn slacks tonight instead of her new dress, she felt goose bumps rise everywhere he touched her. His calloused palm was running over her knee in small circles.

Just then, someone dropped a plate. The shattering sound broke the trance she'd been in. She pulled back and stood from the stool. Grabbing her Coke, she waited until her heart rate leveled.

"I don't know what game you're trying to play, Mr. Callaway, but you won't find any willing participants here. You're better off cutting your losses and moving on. Good night." She turned and walked away, holding her breath until she entered her office. Then she sank down in the couch and tried to get her body back under control.

Half an hour later, she stood and looked out the dark windows and noticed that he was nowhere in sight. She walked back downstairs and continued her nightly ritual. By the time she let herself into her apartment, she was feeling almost normal again.

By the next day, she had convinced herself that the attention he had given her and the way her body had reacted to him was all in her mind. He was here on a mission and would use any means possible to get what he and his father wanted—her property.

She had lain awake for almost an hour wondering why they wanted it so badly.

Boardwalk Bar & Grill sat on the largest lot along what was called the old boardwalk. On either side of the mile-and-a-half-long planked boardwalk, which had been built in the late fifties, sat residence homes, large rental beach homes, and other small businesses. Since Surf Breeze sat on what was essentially an island, land was scarce. The small stretch of land had mostly been owned by the same people for generations.

There were a few smaller hotels along the highway just on the other side of the tall bridge that led to Surf Breeze, but so far the town's lack of space had kept the larger chains away. Most tourists coming into Surf Breeze loved the small feeling. The quaint boardwalk and its nightlife appeal had been a successful mix. That is, up until a few months ago.

Small blue shuttle vans used to run from Emerald Beach to Surf Breeze every hour, but the shuttles had recently been discontinued, and tourism had slowed down. There had been a large uproar from the local business owners, who had petitioned and attended several city hall meetings, but so far, they had not been successful in getting the shuttles running again. Shortly after the shuttles stopped running, the local businesses had been flooded with offers to sell their land or buildings. No one was interested in the businesses, just the property they sat on.

Some of the business owners sold right away. Others were starting to talk about selling. They had gathered and held a meeting at her place a few weeks back, but so far, everyone had been convinced to hold out just a little longer.

She was eating her breakfast—wheat toast and a sliced apple—out on the patio when she heard someone walking up the outside stairs. Turning, she watched Luke open the gate with a white bag and a cup of coffee balanced in his hands.

"What do you want?" she asked, turning back to the local newspaper she'd been scanning.

"Now, is that any way to greet an old friend?" he asked.

"Old friend?" She turned her head and watched him open the tall gate.

"Sure." He smiled. "After all, I brought you donuts and coffee." He set the bag and cup down and then took a seat next to her.

"I already have breakfast." She nodded towards her half-finished toast and apple.

He frowned. "That's not breakfast, that's bird food." He moved her plate aside and pushed the bag of donuts in front of her.

She leaned back and crossed her arms in front of her, noticing that his eyes went to her chest. She

51

had yet to get dressed for work and was wearing shorts and a tank top since it had been surprisingly and wonderfully warm out that morning. She quickly uncrossed her arms when his gaze made her skin feel like it was on fire.

"I don't know why you keep persisting." She took a peek inside the bag and almost moaned when she saw the raspberry-filled delight. Reaching in, she decided that she might as well enjoy it.

The first bite was like heaven. Closing her eyes, she moaned at the richness of the dessert. When she reached for her coffee, he pushed the paper cup in front of her instead. She shrugged her shoulders and took a sip, then frowned.

"Who have you been talking to?" She set the cup down.

He smiled and leaned closer to her. "You have a bit of raspberry"—he used his finger to wipe away some of the jelly from the corner of her mouth—"here." His voice dropped to a low murmur.

She had an image of him talking to her in that tone as he ran his hands all over her. He would coo to her as he told her exactly what he wanted to do to her, what he wanted her to do to him. Shaking her head, she leaned away.

"Well?" she asked again.

He smiled. "I don't know what you mean." He reached into the bag and took out a chocolate-covered donut and took a bite.

"Raspberry-filled donuts, double-chocolate-chip Frappuccino. Have you been talking to my brothers?"

"Brothers? I haven't talked to your brothers." He leaned back as he took a sip of his own coffee.

She crossed her arms over her chest and glared at him as his eyebrows shot up.

He shook his head. "I didn't know you had brothers. Wendy mentioned you had a weakness for the donuts and Frappuccino." He shrugged his shoulders.

"Wendy!" She closed her eyes and swore she'd fire the woman if she weren't such a great asset to her business and a very close friend.

"Don't be too harsh on her. I pestered her enough last night that I'm surprised she didn't give me more information about you." He leaned in, taking another bite of his donut.

"Why are you doing this?" She was really beginning to feel annoyed and stalked.

He chuckled. "I'm attracted to you, Cassey. I thought I saw a spark of attraction in your eyes as well." He shrugged his shoulders and took another sip of his coffee. "I thought we might explore it together."

Honesty was something she hadn't expected from him. Yes, she had been instantly attracted to him; she couldn't deny it. She had noticed it in his eyes as well. But could she trust him? Since she knew she could trust herself to uphold her decision, maybe she could afford to explore a physical relationship. At least for a while.

"I'm not looking for a relationship right now." She frowned as she sipped her coffee.

"Who said anything about a relationship?" He shrugged and looked a little distant.

She leaned back, trying to gauge him. "I suppose I could use a distraction."

She saw his eyebrows shoot up momentarily, but his face and eyes masked his emotions. Then he nodded slowly. "When do you have a night off?"

"Monday."

"Monday is good, but how about tonight?"

"Tonight?" She tilted her head, trying to figure him out.

"Sure, you know, the part of the day that comes just before sunset." He smiled.

"I'll be here tonight."

"Great." He took the last bite of his donut and stood. "I'll see you tonight, then." He reached down and took her hand, pulling her up from her chair, pulling her so close she could feel his heartbeat next to her breasts. He leaned towards her slowly.

She saw the kiss coming, but after his lips touched hers, she realized nothing could have prepared her for the desire that slammed into her. His hands stayed on her hips, holding her close to his body as his mouth explored her own. His rich taste on her tongue caused her to moan and pull him closer as she explored him more. Her hands went into his thick hair, holding him to her until she felt out of breath. Then he pulled back, and she swore she saw a flash of humor in his eyes as he smiled down at her.

"Well, I think we established there is definitely something here."

She tried to smile, but her lips and mind refused to focus. How could a man do this so quickly to her? She felt like a mass of jelly. Gooey all over.

His hands dropped and he stepped away. She thought she saw them shake, but he pushed them deep into his jean pockets before she could be sure. "See you tonight, Cassey." He turned and walked away as she stood there staring after him. When the gate closed, she melted into her chair with a huff, her mind racing.

Her lips still tasted of him. She could still feel his mouth on hers. She closed her eyes and leaned her head back against the chair and wondered just what she had gotten herself into.

Luke spent the next couple of hours in his hotel

room. He was staying in a small place just outside of town. His laptop keys clicked as he answered emails, moved his schedule around, and sent a dreaded email to his father. He clicked the send button and less than five minutes later his cell rang. Knowing it would be his dad, he closed his eyes and sighed. He'd really hoped to put him off for a few hours.

"Hi, Dad," he answered and held the phone away from his ear, waiting for the explosion he knew was coming.

An hour later, with his ear ringing and his head pounding, he showered and dressed to go to Cassey's place. He knew his father wouldn't like the update he'd sent, but he had no idea the old man would threaten to disinherit him if he didn't make this deal happen. Why was Cassey's property so important?

He had more questions now than when he'd been given the assignment, and he knew only one place to get some answers.

As he walked down the boardwalk towards The Boardwalk Bar & Grill, he looked at the other business along the way. There were souvenir shops, small food vendors, an ice cream parlor, even a tattoo shop. Each place had small-town charm. However, some of the businesses sat empty, and their dark windows hung like a cloud over the otherwise happy boardwalk. Cassey's was the largest building and lot along the mile-and-a-half-long strip and the best located. There were tables and chairs sitting outside surrounded by bright flowers in colored wood boxes, making the small patio area look secluded and romantic. Since the weather was turning colder, there weren't any customers dining outside.

When he walked in, the place was almost packed again. If she was struggling with nights like this, he wondered how it used to be and where all her money was going. He knew she had a loan out on the place, but he'd checked the records, and the payments were low enough that she could easily covered them with the traffic she was having. Maybe she owed her family?

He walked up to the bar as Wendy smiled at him. Tonight her top was even lower than the night before and still he found her ample cleavage lacking.

"Back again." She smiled as he nodded. "What'll you have, sweetie."

"Rum and Coke." He turned to look at the place as she went to get his drink. The huge room was separated into two sides. In the back was a stage area with a large dance floor. The dance floor was separated from the dining area by a small half wall. There were two steps leading down to the area, and he had no doubt that the area packed out on nights they had live music.

The other side was the dining area with the bar to the side. There were tall booths that lined the wall and tables in the middle of the floor. The cream-colored tablecloths, along with the lighting and flowers on each table, gave the place an almost rich look. He had to admit, she'd done a great job making the two halves work side by side.

Half an hour and two drinks later, he watched Cassey walk down the stairs. Tonight she wore a silver skirt that hugged her in all the right places. Tall black boots went all the way up to her thighs, and she wore a long net shirt over a silver tank top that flowed just past her belly. She wore silver earrings and jewelry that sparkled in the light. Her long hair flowed down her back in tight curls that looked soft enough to bury his face in.

She walked up to him, and he felt like his tongue had grown three sizes.

"Evening." She smiled and nodded to Wendy, who quickly produced a can of Coke. Cassey leaned on the bar next to him and took a sip.

"You look…amazing," he finally said. Then he pulled her closer and she heard him sniff her neck and hair, no doubt smelling her rich perfume she enjoyed to indulge in. She tensed for a split second, and then relaxed into the embrace.

When she pulled back, she heard Wendy sigh. "You'll excuse me; I have to make my rounds. Wendy…" She waited until her friend walked over. "Get Mr. Callaway anything he wants." She turned and started her nightly ritual. It was still early and the band had yet to show up. She knew it would be an hour before the hectic scurry started. The large back doors opened to the alleyway so that equipment coming and going didn't disturb the diners.

As she walked around the tables, she noticed that there were regular customers scattered around the room. That always made her happy, but new customers were the key to her business. Tourists made up at least seventy percent of the revenue. And in the last few months, she was seeing those numbers dwindle.

By the time she had made it around the room, her feet hurt from her new three-inch high-heeled boots. Oh, they were totally worth the slight pain, but she had to admit she couldn't wait to slide them off and sink down into a nice hot bath.

Late nights had been part of her life since opening the place, and her body was used to the hours. She had more energy than most people did between the hours of seven and one. But it still took a full can of Coke to keep her going; her long-time addiction to the drink helped her mentally get through the later hours.

But tonight she had the extra weight of wondering what would happen after she locked those doors. Looking across the room, she saw Luke leaning against the bar, watching her. The heat that had come from his eyes earlier had seared her. She couldn't remember ever having been looked at like that before. There had been no doubt what he wanted when he saw her walk across the room towards him. She thought that if he could have, he would have marched her up those stairs and back into her apartment. Images of him touching her, what he'd do to her, had flashed into her head ever since they had made their arrangement.

She'd had several relationships in the past, and most had ended amicably. The longest had been Bill, lasting all of five weeks. She knew she had commitment issues. Hell, who wouldn't after living through the horror of her early childhood? She always pulled away before getting too close. She supposed it was because she didn't trust herself to be…well…herself around men.

During any relationship, she would see subtle changes in herself and immediately call it off. They had never been major changes, just little things like using his type of toothpaste instead of hers. Most people would simply overlook things like this, but she couldn't.

She watched Luke turn around and start talking to Wendy. She knew Wendy had gotten her hint about keeping her hands off. They'd been friends ever since she'd hired her that first week. Wendy was one of the only women outside of her family she actually trusted. When she'd heard that Wendy had a similar story to her own, the bond had grown fast and strong.

Luke laughed at something Wendy said, and the sound reverberated through the room. His rich voice was easy to pinpoint in the crowd.

Just then, she received a text saying the band was in the alley, waiting for her to let them in. Walking over to the back doors, she opened them and saw Mike. Mike was the epitome of 80s throwback. She was sure that there had been a time when he had been in many young girls' dreams, but the years hadn't been kind to his hairline or his waistline. But he was a legend for his voice along the whole coastline, and his band played all the right songs and knew how to pack in a crowd.

"How's it going tonight, Cass?" He shifted the large speaker he was holding to hug her.

"Great. We're all ready for you. Tyrone even tells me there's a line growing outside." She propped open the doors to let the rest of the band and all their equipment in.

Less than an hour later, the music started pumping and the crowd was packed in tight. Cassey leaned back against the bar and smiled over at Luke.

Chapter Four

Cassey's smile could light up a room. Luke had the feeling that she didn't do it very often. He had talked to Wendy, trying to gain as much knowledge as he could about her. Wendy wasn't shy when it came to talking about her boss.

He'd found out that she had three brothers, who stopped by frequently. Marcus, the eldest, owned one of the biggest construction companies in town. Roman owned several business as well. Wendy didn't know which ones, but she did mention he drove a new Lexus and always tipped her very well. But Cole was where it got interesting. Cole was one of the most well-known surfers out there. He was a legend, on the cover of every sports magazine and cereal box there was. Luke even thought he'd seen him in the running for man of

63

the year on some magazine cover just last year. When Wendy talked about Cole, her voice grew soft and her eyes turned dreamy. He remembered meeting the man once, years ago, on some beach in Hawaii when Luke had been hiding from his father.

Wendy mentioned there was a sister, but none of the others talked about her. She didn't even know what had happened to her.

He watched Cassey talk to the band and customers, yet he couldn't keep his eyes from wandering over her body. He knew he was in for a long night, so he cut back to sipping a tall beer. He noticed she'd had her Coke in hand for most of the night and smiled.

When the music turned soft, he found her at a table, talking with two young couples. Walking up, he excused her and pulled her onto the dance floor. Just holding her close, smelling her sweet perfume, his mind thought of a million ways to get her upstairs. Just for a moment.

"Any chance I can convince you to take a break?" His hands were running up and down her back as they swayed to the music.

She looked up at him, and her crystal eyes showed him she knew exactly what he meant and wanted the same. "Half an hour."

"Not soon enough." He smiled. "You smell so good." He buried his face into her hair. "I bet you taste even better," he whispered as he dipped and placed his lips on her soft mouth. The taste of her was something he knew he'd never forget, nor want to.

He felt her shake slightly and pulled her tight up against him, making sure that she would feel the desire he had for her. When she moved up against him, he started shaking.

He pulled back and looked into her eyes, noticing that they were out of focus. Her skin glowed and her lips looked darker and fuller than before.

"Luke," she said, her voice soft and sexy, "you make it hard for me to concentrate."

He chuckled. "Good." As the music stopped, he found it hard to release his hold on her so he could step back. They stood in silence for a few seconds as the band announced that they would take a fifteen-minute break. Loud prerecorded music started pumping from the speakers and people around them started bumping to the sounds.

He reached over and grabbed her hand, pulling her towards the narrow stairs. "Perfect timing," he whispered into her ear as he followed her up the stairs, his eyes focusing on what the tight skirt did to her backside as she walked in front of him. When they made it to her office, he pulled her in and pushed her up against the door, his mouth fused to hers.

He felt her breath hitch as her hands grabbed his

hair and held him to her mouth. Her tongue darted out, lapping at his own erotically. His hands moved quickly down from her shoulders, moving lower to rub over the soft mounds, passing her ribs until finally they rested on her hips. His fingers dug into the softness he found there until she moaned. He pushed her legs wide as he stood between those sexy boots. His fingers hoisted up the silver skirt until he found a small black patch of silk covering her. Hearing the material rip, he groaned as he found her silky skin under the soft curls that covered her sex.

Her head fell back against the door as she gasped. Her nails dug into his shoulders as his fingers dove deeper into her moist heat.

"More," he growled as he took her lips again. This time the kiss was fast and a little rough. Her lips were soft under his, moving to keep up with his demands. When her fingers moved to his zipper, he felt like laughing. *Yes!* his mind screamed. Now, it has to be now.

When she freed him and ran her soft hand over his sensitive skin, his eyes closed. He had a moment of clarity as he pushed away and pulled out a condom.

"Here." He shoved the foil package into her hand and watched as she quickly slid it on him. He didn't wait long after she was finished. He pushed her skirt up and buried himself in her in the next second. She gasped and arched her back as he held onto her hips and started to move. With each thrust, he tried to hold onto his control, which was quickly slipping. He'd kept a tight rein on himself in the last day, but now his restraint had completely gone. How could one woman do this to him so quickly?

He felt her inner muscles tighten around him as he leaned in and took her lips again. The soft sounds coming from her mouth caused his control to slip even more. Reaching down, he grasped her soft ass under her skirt and squeezed until he felt her convulse around him. Only then did he allow his own control to break.

Cassey tried to concentrate the rest of the night, she really did. At first, she'd expected Luke to leave within the first half hour after the excitement in her office. How was she ever going to be in that room again without thinking of what he'd done to her? But it was a quarter to closing and he was still sitting at the bar, talking with Wendy, and looking too sexy.

She'd seen the look Wendy had given her when they'd walked down the stairs, no doubt with I-just-had-the-hottest-sex-ever looks on their faces. Wendy had covertly cornered her in the ladies room an hour after their tryst, dying to get the scoop.

"Spill," Wendy said, making sure they were alone in the employee's bathroom.

"Oh my God!" Cassey fell against the sink.

"That good?" she asked as she leaned against the door.

"Better."

"How can it be better? You were only up there fifteen minutes." Wendy looked shocked.

Cassey smiled and shook her head. "The man knows how to use his equipment."

Wendy sighed. "You know, it's been four months since I've had sex. Four months and a lifetime since I've had knock-your-boots-off sex." Wendy frowned.

"It'll happen." Cassey turned and made sure her makeup was still in place and refreshed her lip gloss. "There. Now no one will be able to tell that I've just had OMG sex."

Wendy laughed. "Honey, it's written all over your face. And his." She smiled.

When the last customers had been ushered out by Tyrone, and all the employees had settled their tabs, she locked the doors and turned to see Luke standing by the bar.

"That was some night." He smiled at her. "Are all Fridays like this?"

She shrugged her shoulders. "It was a good night. Not as good as they used to be, though."

His eyebrows shot up. "I hope it's okay that I stayed," he said when she walked towards him.

She nodded since her mouth had gone completely dry. "I'm glad you did," she said, walking into his arms. She wondered what it would take to convince him to spend the rest of the night with her.

"How do you do it?" He wrapped his arms around her waist.

"What?" She tilted her head back, looking into his dark eyes.

"You're a bundle of energy." He chuckled and looked down at his watch. "It's one-thirty and you look as fresh as when you walked down those stairs six-and-a-half hours ago."

"Well," she purred, "I did have a pick-me-up halfway through the night." She smiled as he chuckled.

He started walking her backwards. "Then after what I have planned, you should be ready to run a marathon."

It took too long to climb the back stairs that led to her apartment. She didn't dare make a sound as she unlocked her door and watched as he looked around the small space.

"Nice," he said, before turning to her and gathering her up in his arms. His head dipped, taking her mouth in a long, slow kiss. "Even better," he purred as he backed her towards the hallway. His hands traveled over her, hers over him, releasing hooks and buttons as they walked so that when they finally made it to the bedroom, they were completely naked except for her boots.

She stepped back to slide them off, but he stopped her. "No, leave them." He smiled as he stepped back and looked at her. "My God," he whispered, "you are exquisite."

She felt shy all of a sudden. No one had ever made her feel fluttery inside by just looking at her. He was standing in front of her, naked. His chest was impressive, covered with a light dusting of dark hair, but his six-pack was what caught her eyes and held them. His muscles rippled down his stomach, narrowing downward to his hips. He stood with his legs wide; his thighs were thick and looked strong. Then her eyes moved to his arms again. He had a tattoo on his left bicep, and the dark ink snaked around his arm in a design. When she stepped closer, she noticed that they were waves. Her fingers reached out and touched them.

"Waves?" she asked, looking into his eyes.

He nodded, his dark eyes going even darker. "I lost my brother Calvin a few years back. He was in the Navy." He shook his head, most likely to clear it of the memories.

She stepped closer to him. "I'm sorry." She couldn't imagine what it was like to have a biological sibling, let alone lose them.

He smiled down at her, his fingers running over

the small tattoo she had just above her right hip. "A lily?"

She nodded her head. "My guardian angel." She smiled and pulled his head down towards her. "Later," she moaned as his mouth started demanding speed. This is what she wanted, his hands on her, his mouth on her.

His fingers dug into her hips as he backed her up. Then, when she thought they would fall to the bed together, he turned her so she was facing away from him.

His mouth ran over her shoulders as his hands cupped her breasts. She knew she was smaller upstairs than most women. Hell, Wendy had enough up there for four women. But Cassey didn't discount what she did have. She'd never been ashamed of her body. Even though she was more of a tomboy than her sister, she'd learned a thing or two from Marissa when it came to making men look at her.

Her eyes slid closed as his fingers played down her ribs, past her belly, and found their way into the dark curls covering her sex. Luke's fingers played over her skin, causing her to moan and try to turn around. Now, it had to be now. But his hand held her still. He pushed her shoulders down until she rested her hands on the edge of her bed. Using his feet, he spread her legs wide so her rear end was up in the air.

He ground his hips against her sex until she felt

her legs go weak. Then he used his fingers and spread her even wider. "So beautiful," he whispered just before he slid slowly into her.

Her head jolted back, a gasp of amazement caught in her throat. The zing was instant; his touch just made her want more. His fingers went to her hips and dug in softly as he started to move, pumping in and out of her.

Her fingernails dug into her soft comforter as she focused on his movements. Closing her eyes only heightened the sensation.

She was building too fast. Leaning down, she bit into the comforter, trying to mask the scream that was building.

"Let go," he said softly as his movements sped up. Then he growled as she screamed his name into her mattress.

Cassey was lying face down on her bed, being pinned down. She could feel Luke's breath on her neck. Each exhale caused small bumps to rise on her skin where his breath touched. His left hand was pinned under her hip, his right one in her hair.

"You were wrong." She smiled into the mattress.

"Hmmm?"

"I don't think I could move, let alone run a marathon." She heard him chuckle.

"I guess that makes two of us." He rolled over, pulling her farther onto the bed, closer to him. Her head now rested on his chest, and she realized she still had her boots on.

Sitting up, she quickly unzipped them and tossed them next to the bed.

"I like the boots," he said, smiling as she lay back next to him. "A lot." He ran his hand down her hair.

"I could tell." She smiled to herself. "I like your moves." She held her breath. She'd never felt so awkward before. She'd had sex for just sex plenty of times before, but something was causing her to feel on edge this time.

"Would you mind if I stayed?" he asked softly.

She shook her head. "No, I'd enjoy that." She felt him take a breath, her head rising and falling as his chest moved.

"Good." She heard him sigh. Then his breathing leveled, and she listened to his heart until she could tell he'd fallen asleep.

Thinking her mind would eventually settle, she lay there and thought about the last two days. She was feeling something more than just lust for Luke. How had that happened? They'd only just met. And he was after her bar and grill.

She still didn't trust him not to try and sway her to sell, but she would take what pleasures she could until then. She didn't have a problem keeping her personal feelings locked up. She had hidden herself the first seven years of her life. It wasn't hard to revert back to that.

Besides, she hadn't really allowed herself to get close to anyone in the past, except her family and maybe a few friends.

Moving her head slightly, she looked up at Luke in the dark. His eyelashes rested on his cheeks. He had stubble growing over his chin, which made him look a little dangerous. But it was his eyes that caused her alarm. If she could only see what was behind them, maybe then she would know what card to play next with him.

Usually she could gauge men pretty well, but Luke didn't fit in any of the categories she'd determined that most men fit into. She had yet to find out what his true intentions were, but she knew she enjoyed the physical fun with him. Why not take her pleasures and enjoy it while she waited to find out more about him?

She yawned and snuggled up closer to him. His arms came around her in his sleep. As she closed her eyes, she had to admit that it felt pretty good being held again. It had been too long since she'd felt comfortable enough around someone to sleep next to them all night. When she finally slept, she dreamed of him.

Chapter Five

Luke woke to wonderful smells. Bacon. He looked around and remembered where he was and, more important, who he was there with. A smile crept across his face.

If Cassey ever found out that he'd had one of the best nights of sex in his life, well...He frowned a little. He didn't know what she would do with that knowledge.

Most of the women he'd known would lord it over him, hounding him with it until he caved and gave them whatever they wanted. For some reason, he doubted Cassey would do something like that.

Shaking his head clear, he found his jeans and slipped them on. Following his nose, he walked out on the patio and found Cassey reading the newspaper at the small iron table.

"Good morning." She smiled and he felt something shift inside him. Her smile was something to behold, especially with the colors of the sunrise hitting her hair and face. "I've made you some eggs and bacon." She nodded to a

75

covered plate. "You're just in time."

He sat without saying a word. Picking up the cup of coffee, he took a swallow before speaking.

"You didn't have to, but it smells wonderful." He lifted the lid and smiled when he saw two eggs over easy and three slices of bacon smiling back at him.

While they ate, they talked about the local news. He wasn't familiar with the local happenings in Surf Breeze since he'd been living in Emerald Beach for the last six months, and before that, he'd been in Boston, at school. He tried asking her questions about herself, but she always diverted the conversation away from personal questions.

He knew she only wanted a physical relationship, but he was beginning to hope that the door would be open for something further. He couldn't imagine not wanting her in the future.

When she moved to get up, he quickly took her hand and pulled her closer so they were standing hip to hip.

"What do you say we take a shower before I head out?" he said, leaning down to taste her lips.

"Out?" He could tell she was trying not to ask the unspoken question.

"I've got to run back to Emerald Beach for a day or two. But," he smiled, "I'll be back midday Monday. We have a date, remember?"

She smiled and nodded, and he had a feeling

that she was hiding something behind those eyes. Reaching over, he took her hand in his. She hesitated for a split second and then slowly relaxed.

"I hope you won't be in any trouble with your family over all this." She reached for her coffee with her free hand.

He couldn't help but laugh at the irony. "Trouble? I've been in trouble with my family since the day I was born," he said bitterly. Calvin had been the child his father had always wanted, not him. Sadness threatened to seep in, but he shook it off and looked at Cassey. She was the essence of everything he'd hoped for in life. She was kind, caring, hardworking, smart, and funny. He didn't want his father to tarnish the world she lived in.

Over the next few days, he planned to see exactly what his father had planned for her and her place. It wouldn't hurt to know what he was up against. He was beginning to think he might have to block his father's plans, for her sake. He couldn't describe his feelings for her yet, but he wanted to pursue what was there, and he didn't want his father putting a halt to it before he could decide what it was he wanted.

Cassey was sitting across the table, looking at him like she was trying to figure him out. He shrugged his shoulders.

"Calvin was my father's favorite. I never held it

against him." He smiled, remembering his older brother. "Sometimes you just have to accept your fate."

"What do you mean?" There was a small crease between her eyebrows.

"You know…You've tied yourself into this place, to go into business here with your family's property, while your brothers are off doing their own things, being who they want. When Calvin died, most of my life choices were taken away from me. I went to business school to get the degree my father wanted so I could someday take over the business my great-grandfather, grandfather, and father have spent their lives building." He took another sip of his coffee, which had gone cold. Setting it down, he pushed out of the chair and walked over to a tree that had a wooden bench built around it.

She came up behind him. Her hands went to his shoulders until he turned. "Luke…" She waited until he looked her in the eyes. "We all have choices in life. None of us are destined to do something because someone else demands it. I'm here"—she motioned around her—"because I chose to be. I've worked very hard to get where I am today." She smiled a little. "My heart is here. It's where I belong. If you don't want to be where you are in life, then change it. Don't be something or someone because it's demanded of you."

He smiled and took her shoulders, wishing life were that simple. Leaning down, he placed a soft kiss on her lips. "You are incredible."

She smiled up at him, and he knew that smile would help him get through the next two days.

A few hours later, he parked at Crystal Shores and sat out in his car, looking at the place. It was huge, and it was home. He couldn't remember a time in his life when he hadn't thought of the large white building with all its shiny windows as such.

He leaned back in his seat and frowned. Why couldn't he feel the same way about this place as Cassey felt about her place? He closed his eyes and wondered what would make him feel that much desire in his life. So far, only an image of Cassey's face as she smiled up at him came to mind.

He shook his head clear. Was he beginning to care too much for her? He'd researched her for three months before meeting her face-to-face, so he felt like he'd known her for longer than a few days.

And sex had a way of filling those little gaps in relationships as well. For whatever reason, when he looked into her eyes, he felt like he wanted to be with her longer.

Riding the elevator to the top floor, where his father's office sat on the east side of the tower, he imagined walking into the large room and telling his father he quit. Maybe his father would accept it, hug him, and wish him the best in life. He knew that was never going to happen, so when he walked into his father's office after waiting three minutes for his receptionist to announce him, he held his shoulders back and prepared for the chewing out he knew was coming.

Cassey stood in her office looking down at the almost empty dance floor. She knew that bad nights happened as often as good ones did, but Saturdays always used to be busier than Fridays. Ever since the shuttles had stopped, it was hit or miss.

Over half of her dining floor sat empty as well. Sighing, she crossed her arms over her chest and calculated in her head. She'd been juggling the finances for a few months now. Even with the amount she had in savings, she would be running low a lot sooner than she had previously calculated. She needed those shuttles, or at least for the season to start sooner.

She closed her eyes and leaned her forehead against the one-way glass. There was a call she needed to make, but she'd been dreading it for the last few weeks.

Walking over to her desk, she picked up the phone and dialed her brother's number. Roman picked up on the first ring.

"Hey, sis. What's up?" She could tell he was working outside, something he'd always had a fondness for. He ran his own landscaping business, one of many businesses he owned, and worked a lot with her brother Marcus, who ran his own housing construction company. They were an unbeatable team when it came to new construction in the area.

"Hi, I don't mean to bother you. It sounds like you're working," she said.

She heard him take a breath and step away from the noise. "You are never a bother. Besides, I needed a break."

"I hate to do this, but I'm going to be a little behind on my checks to help out with the home this month. Actually," she sighed, "it might be some time before I can get you the full amount again."

"Are there problems?" She heard the concern in his voice.

"Nothing that I can't handle. Just some setbacks. I'd really hoped to avoid this, especially with the holidays just around the corner." She bit her bottom lip.

"Cassey…" Her brother's voice broke into the calculations she was doing in her head. She was desperately trying to figure out how to get the extra money so she could continue helping her brother with his halfway house. She and her brothers did what they could to financially support the home Roman ran for kids in need. "Don't worry about it. Marcus and I have had a very successful couple of months. We can cover for you until things pick back up." She sighed and closed her eyes as tears started to form. She hadn't expected anything less from her brothers. "If you need anything…"

She shook her head, holding in the emotions. "No, really. I just have a few things to figure out, and then I'll be back in full swing." She smiled. "Thanks, Roman. Tell Marcus thanks, too."

"Sure thing, sis. Well, Marcus is yelling at me to get these damn cabinets in, so I better get back to it. We'll swing by sometime soon."

"I'd like that. See you then." She hung up and walked to the glass and looked down again. If only she could get her numbers back up so she could pay Roman and get rid of this empty feeling in her heart.

The next morning, she walked down the boardwalk before many of the shops opened. There was a bakery at the end of the breezeway that baked the best cinnamon rolls. The rolls were the size of your fist and tasted like heaven. The owners were friends of hers and some of the nicest people she'd ever met. Alfred and Marvin weren't a couple, but they were the closest of friends. They had told her that they'd tried to be more than friends a few years back, but now they just had a working relationship. It seemed to work. The

Lunch Box was the best thing that could have happened to them. Marvin was a recovering coke addict and Alfred had gone through a messy divorce after his wife of twenty years had found out that he was gay. She'd taken his kids, his house, and his heart. The Lunch Box was his one and only love now.

Cassey sat at the outdoor bar as Marvin walked up with a smile. "There's our favorite girl. How's tricks?"

She smiled. "Not bad," she said as he poured her a cup of coffee and set a larger-than-normal cinnamon roll in front of her. Steam rolled off the sticky bun and when the smell of cinnamon and raisins hit her, her mouth watered. Forgoing the coffee for a nibble of the hot roll, she closed her eyes and moaned.

"Marvin, I have said it a million times before, but this is the best thing I've ever had in my life." She took another bite, bigger this time. When her eyes slid open, she looked around. There were fewer than a dozen people sitting around the tables in the small building. She could remember a time when it was a fifteen-minute wait just to get a cup of coffee on a Sunday morning here.

"How are things going around here?" She frowned a little.

"Don't worry about us; we're doing just fine. We paid the bank off last year and anything we make just pads our pockets. You on the other hand..." He frowned as she took a sip of her coffee. "We're worried about you. We know where your money goes and..."

She held up her hand, shaking her head. "It's fine. Roman and Marcus are helping out right now." She smiled as relief crossed Marvin's face.

"We'd sure hate to see anything happen to that place. All the good you four have done." He shook his head and smiled.

When she was done eating her breakfast, she walked towards the small mall area where there were clothing shops. Deciding that tomorrow night called for a new dress, she took her time picking out the perfect outfit. A few hours later, she found what she was looking for. The dress was perfect. Its teal lace set off her eyes and skin tone perfectly. Not to mention she already had a pair of heels that matched the cheery color.

She took her time walking back down the boardwalk. It was just past noon and almost every place was open. She took her time stopping at each shop, talking to the owners or workers for a while and enjoying her time.

She really did feel like part of a community here. It was wonderful how close everyone was. There had never been animosity between businesses owners. Everyone was kind and generally concerned about keeping the boardwalk flowing with tourists.

She knew a few of the local kids and always

knew when they'd ditched school during the week because most of them hung out at the beach. Walking over to a group she knew well, she smiled at Bobby, the leader.

"How's it going?" she asked as she leaned back against the railing of the walkway. Looking out towards the beach, she saw that the sand was almost empty. There were a few joggers and several families braving the cooler weather but nothing like during the season.

"Oh, hey, Cass." He lightly put an arm around her. He'd grown almost a foot since last summer and now she had to crane her neck just to look into his blue eyes. His unruly brown hair was falling in his face, a face that most high school girls would fall for immediately.

"I heard you got onto the soccer team this year," she said with a proud smile on her face. Two of Bobby's friends chuckled, so she raised her eyebrows at them in question.

"We all did," Steve, the shortest of the three, said. "By default. There wouldn't be enough kids for a whole team if he hadn't dragged us along for tryouts."

"Well, I still think it's wonderful you all are going to play." She smiled and patted Bobby's arm. She knew Bobby's history, which was much like her own. He'd been put in the system when he was five after his father had put him in the hospital by pouring scalding water all over his little body.

Taking part in Roman's charity, the Spring Haven Home for Boys, had its ups and downs. Watching Bobby grow and become a trusted young man in town had been a perk. She'd seen him grow so much since he'd been placed in the home run by her brother.

"Well, I'd better get going. Let me know when your first game is. I'd love to cheer you on."

He nodded and smiled, looking a little embarrassed. She turned and walked towards her place, a smile on her face and her heart lifted.

When she walked in, she didn't expect to see Luke sitting at the bar, but there he was, dressed in khaki jeans and a short-sleeved shirt. His leather jacket was tossed over another chair as he talked with Wendy, laughing at something she'd said.

She smiled and walked over to him. "Well, this is a surprise." He turned and faced her upon hearing her voice. His smile grew wider.

"We were just talking about you," Wendy said before moving down the bar to fill an order.

"Oh?" She turned to Luke.

"Only good things, I swear." He put his hands on her hips and pulled her closer. He buried his face in her neck and took a deep breath. "There," he sighed, "now I feel better."

When she pulled back, she thought she saw a flash of something in his eyes. Was it sadness? It was gone just as quickly as it had crossed his face.

"I wasn't expecting you until tomorrow." She smiled and enjoyed the feeling of being close to him.

"I finished with my meetings earlier than expected and wanted to be here, instead." He smiled. "Have you had lunch?" She shook her head. "Great." He smiled and nodded to an empty table. "Why don't we eat someplace close?"

She smiled. "I hear they have the best calamari and coconut shrimp."

"Count me in." He took her hand and then noticed the bag she'd set down. "Shopping?"

She smiled as she nodded. "I'll just drop this off upstairs and be right back." She rushed up the stairs to her office. Taking a few deep breaths, she tried to calm her nerves as she reapplied some makeup and lip gloss. When she walked down the stairs, she felt more in control.

He was sitting in one of the larger booths along the back wall. The window overlooked the boardwalk and beach. It was one of her favorite spots. He had ordered her a frozen Pineapple Sunset, one of their signature specialty drinks, and he sipped a tall beer.

"I ordered us some calamari and shrimp for starters. I'm thinking of having some fish tacos. What about you?"

"You can't go wrong with Sam's tacos. I absolutely love the Mahi Mahi po' boy. We boast having the best along the Gulf." She sat next to him in the booth and took a sip of her drink. She realized how good it felt to sit in her own place and enjoy the atmosphere.

Luke put his arm around her and pulled her closer. "There…" He smiled at her. "Now I can relax."

She smiled and looked around. "You know, I've never been on a date in here before," she said absentmindedly.

"Really?" He looked around with her. "It's a great place. Comfortable." He tilted his head, like he was thinking about something. "If the food is as good as you say, I see no reason for you to be struggling."

She sighed and rested her chin on her hands. Bella, one of her waitstaff, delivered their appetizers.

"I'm struggling, we all are, because the shuttles stopped," she said as she scooped up some sauce with her calamari. The rich flavors hit her tongue, causing her a moment of pure pleasure.

"Shuttles?" He looked at her, a frown on his lips. "No, they didn't."

Her eyebrows shot up. "Of course they did. About two months ago, just after the busy season." She watched as he took some calamari and sampled.

"I'm pretty sure they didn't. At least not from

Crystal Shores." He frowned as he sampled the shrimp next. "This is wonderful." He took another bite.

"I was lucky to get Sam." She nodded and grabbed one of the larger shrimp and allowed the bite to melt on her tongue. The juices, the spices— everything about it was perfection. Closing her eyes for a split second, she sighed and enjoyed the tastes. When she opened her eyes, Luke was looking at her funny. His eyes heated, watching her mouth as her tongue darted out to lick some of the tangy sauce from her lips. She knew that look but wasn't prepared for the heat that spread throughout her body by just seeing his reaction to her.

The spell was broken when the waitress walked up and interrupted. After they had placed their lunch orders, Luke looked over at her and frowned a little.

"You said something about the shuttles stopping?"

She sighed. She really didn't want to talk business, not when the looks he was giving her were causing her insides to boil. But she could tell the mood had passed and he was all business now.

She nodded and took another sip of her drink.

"That just doesn't make sense. It's not the hotels that run the service, but the counties." He frowned a little more and took a drink of his beer. "After all, it benefits everyone." She could tell he

89

was deep in thought, so instead of commenting, she watched as his mind whirled, working it out. She knew the conclusion he'd come to; she'd come to the same conclusion a few weeks back. It took him almost five minutes to work it all out in his head before he said anything more to her.

"You know, there are several hotel owners that sit on high places on the county board. Some are appointed, others voted in." He frowned a little more and she smiled. "My father is one of those." He stopped talking when the waitress dropped off their lunch.

She took a bite of her po' boy and watched him absentmindedly take a bite of his burger. "You know," he said, setting down the burger, "if I wanted to buy out business land for cheap, first thing I'd do is find a way to make sure the land wasn't worth much." He picked up a fry and dipped it in catchup.

"Great minds think alike," she said, under her breath.

"What?" He set down his burger and looked at her.

She shook her head and took another bite of her sandwich.

"You think that's what my father is doing?" he asked, looking a little hurt.

She shrugged her shoulders. "You tell me. You're the one walking into my place with an offer that's three times lower than what this place is worth."

She saw the shock on his face and recognized the second realization hit him. He looked hurt, genuinely hurt, and for the first time, she thought that maybe she'd misjudged him.

Chapter Six

Luke took another sip of his beer, but it tasted sour now. He should have known that his father would stoop to a low like this. After all, his great-grandfather had won the hotel in a card game over eighty years ago.

His family was full of bottom-of-the-barrel scum. He had an uncle who just couldn't keep his hands to himself and was on his seventh wife, one that was under half his own age.

When he looked across the table at Cassey, his blood began to boil. How could his family have done something so terrible to someone so sweet? He reached for her hand and felt it shake in his own. "Cassey, I know coming from me it's probably not much, but I'm sorry."

Her eyebrows shot up. "You're sorry? Why are you sorry?"

He looked down at their joined hands and shrugged his shoulders. "For my father. For my family. For what they've done to you, to your business." He shook his head in disgust.

"Luke..." She waited until he looked up into those gray eyes of hers before continuing. "You had nothing to do with this. I can see that clearly. You have nothing to apologize for."

He dropped her hand, feeling disgusted with himself. There was more he had to tell her, but looking around, he knew this wasn't the time or the place.

Picking up his burger, he took another bite and starting talking about the food and how wonderful it was. He could see that she knew he was trying to change the conversation and after a few minutes, she gave up on trying to convince him of his lack of guilt.

"So..." He leaned a little closer to her, picking up her hand again in his. Her hands were small and soft, and he wanted to hold on to them as long as he could. "Tell me a little more about yourself. What do you like to do in your off time?"

She looked at him funny and then smiled. "I thought you would already know most everything about me." She nodded towards the bar. "I know Wendy can be quite the talker, and," she sighed, "I figured you would have a thick file on me from your father."

He shrugged. "You can't learn everything about someone from a file and word of mouth."

She smiled at that. He was getting used to those quick little turns of her lips. He had the feeling she didn't do it very often, so he enjoyed each little twitch.

"Well, I'm twenty-five this spring. I have three brothers and a sister. I was raised by the most caring people on the planet who occasionally acted like they still lived in the sixties." She smiled a full smile at this, and her eyes sparkled in the dim light of the dining room. "Their daughters were more like my sisters who helped raise us all. Even when my brothers drove us all nuts, they showed us nothing but love and patience." She blinked a few times and her smile dropped. "I worked myself through a few years of night school, got my degree, and opened this place." She reached for her drink.

"What about your sister?" He watched her eyes go misty and saw her whole body tense.

"She left us shortly after her seventeenth birthday." She looked down at her hands. "We haven't heard from her since."

"It must have been wonderful having such a large family." He knew she was grateful for the change of the subject.

She nodded. "Tell me about your brother."

Now it was his turn for his eyes to turn a little sad. "Calvin was my complete opposite." He sighed and leaned back. The only way to gain her trust was to give her a little in return. "He was everything my father wanted in a son. My mother, too. He was helping my father run the hotel by the age of eighteen. After a few years of college, he shocked us all by joining the Navy." He smiled a little, remembering how his brother had stood up to his father to fight for his country. "He served two years before the accident. He worked in the engine room. The accident killed four people."

She reached over and took his hand, again. He could see the sadness in her eyes. "I'm so sorry."

He smiled and nodded. "So, after Calvin was gone, my father turned his eyes for the first time in my direction. I was pulled out of my college and sent to a more prestigious college for a business degree so I could one day take over the empire." He dropped her hand and took a swallow of his warm beer.

"I'm sure your parents are proud of you."

He laughed. "Sure they are. I'm told constantly what a joy I am to them both."

Just then, the waitress walked up and cleared the empty plates. After she left, Luke looked at Cassey. Her hair was tied back in a loose braid. Her shirt and slacks looked comfortable, and he realized it was the first time he'd seen her in everyday clothes. He liked seeing the more relaxed look on her; it suited her, somehow, just as the tight dress and killer heels had.

He leaned closer to her, getting a good whiff of her perfume. The sweet scent flooded his mind with images of her lying naked underneath him. "How much time do we have before you need to be on shift again?"

Her gray eyes turned a little darker. "I guess that depends on what you had in mind," she purred.

He grabbed her hand, tossed a handful of bills on the table for the waitress, and pulled her towards the back stairs.

She laughed as he pulled her up the stairs. "Luke, slow down." He felt her breathing hard as they reached the back door, and she pulled out her keys.

He pinned her against the wall next to the door and kissed her until he was breathless as well. Her hands went into his hair, holding him to her as they quickly explored each other. Finally, he pulled away and grabbed the keys from her. "Hurry," she said as he slid the key into the lock and opened her front door.

Then she was pushing him against the wall, using her hands to pull off his shirt and loosen his jeans. His fingers wouldn't work fast enough as he fumbled and pulled off her clothes. When their clothes were on the floor, she pulled him down the hall towards her bedroom.

They made it to the room just as the last piece of clothing hit the floor. She laughed and pulled away, walking slowly over to the bed. Her hair was a mess from his hands, her eyes looked heated, and he'd never seen her look more beautiful than right now.

She lifted a finger and wiggled it towards him. "Come and get me." Her tongue darted out to lick her bottom lip and he couldn't stop himself from moving towards her.

When he reached her, she pulled his hands together in one of hers, holding them away from her body. "Oh, no. This time, I want complete control." She motioned for him to step closer, still lightly holding his hands.

"Anything you want." He looked into her eyes, and part of him believed he would give her just that. Anything.

A smile flashed on her lips quickly and then was gone as her eyes heated even more. "Lie back." She motioned towards the bed. He positioned himself with his hands resting behind his head.

"I'm ready." He smiled, watching her eyes zero in on his erection. He was, indeed, ready. Her tongue darted out and licked her lips again, causing him to moan.

Then she was sliding up on the bed, her thighs wrapped around his hips as she hovered above him, looking down at his face.

"Stay still." She leaned down and placed a kiss along his collarbone. He closed his eyes and enjoyed the feel of her exploring him. Her fingers ran over his arms and chest, followed closely by her mouth and tongue. When she reached his navel, he held his breath as her fingers lowered and grasped him lightly. He moaned as she explored his length slowly. When her head dipped down, and she took him fully into her mouth, his hands went into her hair, holding her.

"Utt, utt." She tsked and shook her head, pulling back until she looked at him. "Hands behind your head." She smiled.

"Yes, ma'am." He moved his hands back, knowing it was going to kill him not to touch her. She waited until he was settled again before dipping her head back down to finish her task. He'd never been dominated so wonderfully before. She used her mouth and fingers to guide him to the brink of losing control. She must have felt him on the edge, because she sat up, quickly pulled a condom from her nightstand, and rolled it on him. Then she climbed up, her knees on either side of his hips as she sank down slowly onto him. His hands went to her hips, holding her still as he felt her inner muscles clamp around his arousal.

When he looked up at her, her eyes were closed. Her head was thrown back as she moaned with pleasure.

"More," he said, digging his fingers into her soft skin to get her to move on him. Her hips moved slightly, rotating with her pleasure as she began to move over him.

His mind, his body, every part of him focused on not losing control, giving her pleasure before taking his own. He reached up and ran his fingertips down her sensitive skin until he felt her speed pick up. When he reached the sensitive spot between her legs, he felt her stiffen around him as she cried out his name.

She melted down on top of him. Using his hips, he twisted until she was underneath him. He looked down at her face; her eyes were closed and her sweet mouth was slightly opened. Remembering how it felt wrapped around his cock, he flexed his back, sliding deeper into her wetness.

"Again," he growled. "I'll have that again."

Her eyes blinked open, and he saw that they were clouded with desire. When his speed picked up, he watched her face flush and her eyes heat as her nails bit into his shoulders. Their breath was labored as they lost themselves together.

Cassey stood in her shower and let the hot water soothe her sore muscles. She'd expected that by controlling the situation, she would have kept him at a distance. Instead, it had allowed him to get further into her head.

She'd never meant for this relationship to be anything other than physical. She couldn't afford to let it. After all, his family was trying to take everything she'd ever worked for. No one was ever going to make her feel inferior again. She had spent so much time training herself not to feel useless. Not that he made her feel that way, just a little frustrated. She was still unsure of Luke's real intentions. She was enjoying the physical aspects of their relationship. Who wouldn't? But underneath it all, there were always questions about his real motives.

She believed him when he talked about his family, but she knew that wouldn't stop him from fulfilling a family obligation. Especially when it meant his whole future. Knowing she had only a while longer to enjoy being with him, she was determined to make the most of every second she had. She really was enjoying playing the game.

She sighed, remembering what they had just done, and reached for the shampoo just as the shower door opened. She stopped herself from screaming, just barely.

He laughed and stood there naked, looking at her. "Sorry, didn't mean to scare you."

She shook her head. "You didn't." She knew it was ridiculous, but her chin went up in defense.

He laughed again as he stepped into the shower and shut the glass door. "I bet you've watched *Psycho* too many times."

She shrugged her shoulders. "Who hasn't?"

He laughed again, taking some shampoo and dumping it on her head. Using his fingertips, he started massaging her scalp. Her eyes closed and her entire body went lax. This was her one weakness.

"You like that, huh?" she heard him whisper next to her ear, causing goose bumps to rise up on her body.

She nodded. "Hmmm, yes."

"Here…" He took her hands and placed them on the shelf in her shower. "Hold on." Using his hands, he moved her closer to the wall, allowing himself more room behind her.

Her eyes closed as she leaned forward. The water dripped over her shoulders and down her back as he ran his soapy hands down the same path. Finally, his fingers touched her sensitive skin, sending a shock wave up her body until her fingertips felt numb.

He squeezed some more soap into his hand and ran it lightly over her curls until she heard the slick sound of soap mixed with her arousal.

She felt him slide slowly into her until he was so deep that she felt his every heartbeat. She moaned as his hands ran over her breasts, and he used his fingers to pinch her nipples slightly. She felt herself building, her toes curling as her legs started shaking.

"Go ahead," he whispered next to her ear. "Let go."

She couldn't have stopped herself if she'd wanted to. His warm mouth was next to her skin as she cried out and gripped the shelf so tight, her fingers turned white.

Chapter Seven

It was just past one when they climbed back up the stairs to her apartment. It had taken him three Cokes just to keep his eyes open until closing time. Cassey, on the other hand, looked like she'd just woken up.

"I still don't know how you do it." He shook his head as they walked into her apartment, his overnight bag tossed over his shoulder.

She laughed. "Years of practice. I've been living this schedule since the year before I graduated high school." She walked over and opened the glass doors that led to her patio.

The rain had started to fall almost an hour ago, which had caused the club to fill up as everyone rushed to get off the boardwalk. He tossed his bag down on her bed and walked over behind her. Wrapping his arms around her, he watched as the sky lit up with lightning.

She sighed and rested back into his chest. "I always love fall around here. The crazy storms, the cooler weather." She sighed again.

"I bet it doesn't hurt that things slow down a little either."

She turned in his arms, wrapping her hands around his neck. "That, too." She leaned up and placed a kiss on his lips. "You look beat. I'm glad you decided to stay here tonight instead of going back to your hotel."

He smiled down at her. "Me, too. Plus, we still have our date tomorrow. Remember?"

She smiled and nodded. "Yes, I'm looking forward to it."

He had the feeling she was hiding something from him. The statement didn't reach her eyes, and for a split second, he thought she was lying. But then she was pulling him towards her bed and removing his clothes, and he forgot all about the look she'd given him.

The next day they walked hand in hand along the boardwalk. She was taking him to a local place for breakfast. She wore a pair of light-colored pants and a cream-colored top with a light jacket on. The rain had stopped just before sunrise, and he could tell it was going to be warm enough today that they could really enjoy themselves.

"Here we are." She stopped in front of a small breakfast place. The red and white stripes on the awnings and the black-and-white tiled floors, made the place look vintage. They walked in and sat on the bar stools, and she ordered two cinnamon rolls and two cups of coffee.

He watched her chat with one of the owners as she drank her coffee and waited for a fresh batch of rolls from the oven. She looked comfortable here, chatting among the locals.

When some local kids came walking in just after they had been served, she walked over to them and scolded them for not being at school already. He almost laughed at how motherly she was towards them. She knew each kid by name and even talked to them about sports.

Finally, the kids took their breakfast to go and promised that they were heading to school. Cassey looked relieved when she sat back down to finish her roll.

"What was that all about?" he asked, trying to figure her out.

She shrugged her shoulders. "Bobby is a good kid."

He waited and when she didn't finish, he asked, "And why do you have such an interest in whether he's at school or not?"

She laughed. "Because he's a handful, and he's one of my brother's kids."

107

His eyebrows shot up. "I didn't know you had a nephew." He turned to watch the kid walk down the boardwalk.

"No," she chuckled. "I don't. My brother runs a halfway house of sorts. Kind of like my parents did, but on a larger scale." She nibbled on the last bite of her roll. He had finished his already and was trying not to order another one. Instead, he sipped his coffee and dreamed about another roll.

"Which brother?"

"Roman. He bought an old house in downtown Spring Haven, right off the bay. Marcus, Cole, and he rebuilt the place shortly after high school. Then"—she shrugged her shoulders—"he started taking kids in."

He shook his head. "Isn't there a lot to that kind of thing?"

She laughed. "You have no idea what he had to go through the first two years. Ready?" She stood up and waved bye to her friends.

"Sure." He took out his wallet to pay, but she shook her head.

"Not around here." She smiled and nodded. "Alfred and Marvin will be upset if you pay for anything."

"Alfred and Marvin?"

"The owners. It's a standing rule on the boardwalk between us owners."

"Seriously?" He stopped walking just outside the door and looked down at her. "You don't charge anyone and they don't charge you?"

She smiled and nodded. "We're a family. You don't charge family."

She took his hand as they started walking up the boardwalk. When they reached the railing, she leaned against it and closed her eyes and took a deep breath.

"I love it here." She spun around, resting her back against the railing as she looked at him. "There is always something to do, people to watch." She nodded to an old couple passing them. They were dressed in matching bright red shirts and shorts. Cassey smiled and waved to them. "So, what do you want to do?"

He looked down at her and smiled. When she saw the look in his eyes, she chuckled. "We can do that again later. I mean what do you want to see along the boardwalk first?"

"It's your neighborhood. What do you want to show me?"

She grabbed his arm and started pulling him down the walk, a smile playing on the edge of her lips. "I know where we'll go first. You'll love it." He followed her willingly down the walk. She entered a large blue building with a sign that said "Boardwalk Arcade" in neon above the door.

He stopped her just inside the doors and smiled

down at her. "Really? An arcade?"

She laughed. "It's much more than just an arcade. Come on." She tugged his arm again.

Three hours later, he was not only exhausted, but starving again. She'd run him through the laser tag arena three times, each time kicking his butt until finally he'd caved and asked if they could try the go-carts outside. He was proud when he'd lapped her small red go-cart, and he'd finally beat her at something. He'd convinced her to run another round, this time on the slick track where he annihilated her once again.

They played a round of miniature golf and tied, then went inside to order a slice of pizza and a Coke. They ate at a large picnic table outside under an awning, and he couldn't remember ever having this much fun on a first date.

They laughed and joked with each other over the pizza, and then she pulled him into the arcade again. They won enough tickets between them to get a large stuffed dog, which she carried down the boardwalk proudly.

By the time they walked through the doors of her place, his mind was made up. He was going to tell his father next time he saw him that his new scheme wouldn't work and, more important, he would have nothing to do with it.

When Cassey walked into her place with the large, stuffed dog on her hip, she couldn't help but smile. She couldn't deny it, even to herself; she'd just had the best day since...well, since she could remember.

Being with Luke was easy, almost too easy, but she wasn't going to think about that just yet. The place was pretty empty, which was to be expected on an out-of-season Monday. But it was even more empty than she'd come to expect. She wasn't too worried since her brothers weren't expecting anything extra from her for a while. Still, it would have been nice to pay the bank the extra she'd gotten used to paying. If she could have stuck to her plans, she would have had them paid off in less than five years. Now, however, she was looking at adding at least a few months to that.

"I hope you aren't planning on skipping out on me for dinner," he said next to her ear, causing little bumps to rise down her neck.

Shaking her head, she turned back and smiled at him. She found herself doing that more often around him, and it was almost becoming natural. There had been few other men in her life that had made her smile this much—her brothers, an occasional boyfriend—but no one had ever made her feel this young. Even as a kid, she hadn't felt this carefree.

"I just want to shower and change first," she said, waving to Wendy as they walked by.

"A shower sounds good." The way he said it had her mind whirling and heat spreading throughout her entire body.

She stopped on the first step and turned to him. "Maybe I'll let you wash my back, again." She wrapped her arms around his shoulders as he leaned up and placed a soft kiss on her lips.

"Mmm." He wrapped his hands around her waist and pulled her closer. She felt his desire pressing against her hip, and her pulse jumped at the thought of him inside her.

Smiling, she turned and rushed up the stairs, holding his hand and pulling him along quickly.

After the shared shower and some very steamy sex, Luke left her alone in the bathroom to get ready for dinner. For the first time that day, she had a moment to herself.

Her mind played over the time spent with him in the last few days. Maybe she was building him up to be something bigger than he was in her mind. She tried to be as rational as she could, remembering how he'd treated her, how she was around him. She kept coming back to the fact that all she could think about was spending more time with him.

By the time she was dressed and ready for an evening out, she was determined to enjoy the time she had with him, no matter what.

He surprised her by walking her to his car, an older model classic, which he said he'd rebuilt with a buddy of his a few years back. When she sat on the leather seats, she felt like she was riding in a new car instead of one built in the early sixties.

She hadn't planned on him driving towards Emerald Beach, or on them going to Crystal Shores for dinner. She'd never been to his family's hotel before, nor had she ever been to a restaurant quite this fancy before. She felt a little out of her element when the maître d' looked her over as they walked in.

"Good evening, Mr. Callaway," the man said with a slight accent. "I trust your drive was pleasant."

"Yes, thank you, Andre." Luke took hold of her hand as they followed the man to a secluded table near the bay windows.

After they were seated, Luke ordered some wine and they were left alone to look over the menus. She set hers down and looked across the table at Luke.

"Why didn't you tell me you were taking me here?" She noticed how comfortable he looked sitting in a room that, to her, felt stuffy and made her feel under-dressed.

He shrugged his shoulders. "I didn't think it would really matter." She could see that he was telling the truth. To him, this was just another place to dine. To her it felt like sleeping with the enemy. Then again—she chuckled a little—she really *was*

113

sleeping with the enemy. It didn't really matter either way; she was going to enjoy the rest of their night together.

"So, tell me what's good to eat here," she said, picking up her menu again and looking over it. She tried not to gasp when she noticed the prices. She could just imagine how empty her place would be if her prices were this high.

"The lobster and shrimp are my favorite, but the chef makes some really great pork chops." He smiled across the table at her, and she remembered that he had looked just as excited to have a slice of cold pizza for a couple bucks at lunch.

"You surprise me," she said, setting down her menu again. When he raised his eyebrows and just looked at her, she continued. "You give off the impression that you're a beer-drinking, pizza-eating kind of guy, but then you take me here." She motioned around to all the people wearing clothes that cost more than her entire wardrobe had and to the dining room that would bring in more in one night than she brought in the bar and grill in a whole week. "And yet you fit in here. More than that, you were born for this." She heard herself say those words, and for a split second, her heart skipped.

Her mind screamed at her, wondering what she was doing messing around with someone like Luke Callaway.

He was looking at her kind of funny, and then

he smiled. "You know, I've never really thought of this place as anything but home. Where most people can't see beyond the pressed table cloths and high-priced food, all I see is myself as a teenager"—he nodded to a back table area—"back at that table doing my homework with my brother and eating three meals a day either in the kitchen or at an empty table because our parents were too busy to make dinner or take us home." She watched as a sad look crossed his face.

She'd never thought about it like that. She started wondering what it would be like if she started a family. Would she be any different than his parents had been? Would her kids be forced to sit in a booth and waste their childhoods because she was too busy running her business?

Shaking her head, she tried to push those thoughts to the back of her mind. She'd never thought about having a family of her own, not until today. She wasn't ready for a family or, at this point, ready to commit to someone for more than a few weeks at a time.

Chapter Eight

Luke wasn't sure what had changed during dinner, but the whole atmosphere had changed from light and friendly to quiet and solemn. It didn't help matters that, shortly after they had ordered, his father had showed up at their table. He was sure that Andre had called upstairs and notified him of their arrival.

"Luke, I heard you were down here." He stood to shake his father's hand. He and his father had never really been on friendly terms, especially not since Calvin's death.

"Yes, sir. May I introduce Cassey Grayton. Cassey, this is my father, Jeffery Callaway."

"How do you do?" His father shook Cassey's hand. He could see a shocked and somewhat

117

cornered look on Cassey's face. He would have done anything to remove it and replace it with the smiles she'd given him all day.

"How do you do. You have a lovely place here," Cassey said stiffly.

"Thank you. I won't keep you from your meal." His father turned towards him. "Luke, can I have a word with you?"

Luke looked towards Cassey, who nodded quickly.

He followed his father into the back office area and felt the full force of his father's anger after he shut the door.

"What are you doing?" His father was just an inch shorter than him, but the man still had the power to make him feel like he was only three feet tall.

"I'm enjoying a dinner date. You did say you wanted me to try any means possible." He crossed his arms and held his breath.

"I didn't expect you to bring that woman here." His father started pacing. Jeffery Callaway never did anything idle; the fact that he was pacing didn't escape Luke's attention.

"Really?" He leaned slightly against the closed door. "When you give me a job to do, you should trust me enough to complete the task on my own terms. However, since handing me this task, you have done nothing but interfere." He stood up when his father stopped pacing right in front of him, and then he watched his face start to turn a dark shade of red. "If you're finished, I have a date waiting." Luke turned and left the room without another word.

As he walked back to the table, he tried not to dwell on the fact that his father was an ass. He was determined to enjoy the rest of the evening, regardless of what his father thought of him or Cassey.

Cassey seemed to enjoy her meal, but instead of ordering dessert or drinks after they finished their plates, he quickly paid. Then he pulled her out the back glass doors that led past the large tropical pool. There were low lights strung around the palm trees, and soft music was playing from the hidden speakers, but he didn't stop yet. Instead, he pulled her past the iron gates and onto the beach. Pausing so she could remove her shoes, he toed off his dress shoes and rolled up his pants. She laughed a little and helped him so the sand and water wouldn't destroy them.

"Here, we can leave our shoes here." He walked over to a small bush area just outside the iron gate.

She looked around questioningly.

He laughed. "I've been hiding my shoes here all my life, and I've never had a pair stolen." She smiled and nodded and set her sexy heels next to his black shoes.

119

Then she took his hand as they started walking down the long strip of beach. He always loved the feel of the white sand under his feet. His resort had been raking the sands for as long as he could remember. Here, you were in no danger of being stuck by a broken shell or a wayward glass bottle.

He sighed when they made it to the water's edge. Since it was fall, the water was cool and when it lapped at their feet, they both gasped then giggled.

"Maybe we'll avoid the water." She rushed from the edge, pulling him along. The walked for a while in silence, their hands lightly grasped together, swaying next to them.

"Your father seemed nice," she said offhandedly.

A bark of laughter escaped his lips.

"What?" She pulled his hand until he stopped and looked at her.

Shaking his head, he looked down at her. "Let's not spoil the evening by talking about my father." He pulled her closer, noticing how her silver eyes sparkled in the moonlit. He brushed her hair out of her face when the light breeze pushed it in her eyes.

"You look lovely tonight." He pulled her closer. "The way your hair shines in the light." He pushed a strand of her hair out of her face again. She'd curled it tonight, leaving the long strands in little loops down its length. The strapless dress she'd worn allowed her hair to fall lightly on her bare shoulders. His fingers trailed down her hair until he felt her soft skin under his hands. Running a finger lightly over her shoulder, he watched as her breath hitched. Her chest rose and fell lightly, causing his eyes to follow the slight movements.

He was transfixed as he watched her head fall back a little. Her eyes closed slightly and she held her breath as his fingers played over her skin. He ran a finger up her neck until he couldn't stop himself, and he dipped his head to taste the soft skin where his fingers had just been.

He felt her moan against his lips, and the sound vibrated along his hands as they ran up her back. The softness of her dress, her skin, almost undid him. It took all his will to pull away and start walking down the beach again.

They came upon a little shack along the beach that sold Italian ice and sat at the bar stools and enjoyed the cool treat. He'd been eating at the small business for as long as he could remember, yet he didn't even know who owned the place. He knew that if the hut had been along Cassey's boardwalk, she would know the owners and their whole life stories, as well. He wondered exactly what that said about him as a person.

"This is incredible," Cassey said, breaking his deep thoughts. He smiled over at her. "I've never had Italian ice before; it's basically ice cream, right?"

He chuckled. "It's actually closer to sorbet. He held up a spoonful of his favorite, pina colada. "Here, try this one."

He watched as she took his spoon into her mouth and closed her eyes. "Yum." Her tongue darted out to lick her bottom lip. "That's as good as the raspberry."

He smiled and nodded. "Calvin's favorite was raspberry."

She smiled. "My sister, Marissa, loved pina colada. My brothers always had one favorite, orange." She chuckled. "It's funny, they could never agree on what to have for dinner, or to drink, but always agreed on orange sorbet."

"I'd like to meet them sometime," he blurted out before he knew what he was doing. He didn't know what had caused him to say it and didn't even know if he really did want to meet them. But the more time he spent with Cassey, the more time he wanted to spend with her.

He understood their arrangement, that it was just physical. He really wasn't looking for a long-term relationship, especially one he already knew his father wouldn't approve of. Not that he needed his father's approval to date a woman. Hell, if he thought about it, he *wanted* a woman his folks didn't approve of. But there was already so much his father was up in arms about. Most of it was his fault, some of it wasn't, but he was sure his father would find a way to blame him for them anyway.

He sighed and tried to focus on the now instead of the old arguments with his father.

"Where did you go?" she asked when he blinked and cleared his mind.

"Hmm?" He tried to recover by taking another nibble of his sorbet.

She leaned on the counter and gave him an I'm-not-buying-it look. He was sure he could get out of explaining himself, but then he sighed again and caved.

"I had an argument with my father earlier. I was just thinking about how he always blames me for everything."

"I'm sure he doesn't blame you for everything."

He chuckled. "Do you always look at the bright side of things?"

She shook her head. "No, but you must have had some wonderful times growing up."

"I did. My brother was the best part. Calvin shielded me from most of my parents' wrath. He's the one that taught me how to throw a football, encouraged me to ask Tammy Lynn out in fifth grade, bought me my first box of condoms." He smiled. "He also taught me how to drive and passed on his love of classic cars." He took a drink from the water bottle he'd ordered. "If I think about it, all the great moments in my life happened because of my brother."

"I would have loved to have met him." She'd leaned her face in her hands on the counter and was listening to him like in a daydream. "My brothers played a huge part in my great memories too." She laughed, and sat up. "They taught me not to be gullible, to work hard for what you want, and to never back out of a fight."

"Okay, now you're going to have to explain all those." He chuckled.

She smiled as she finished the last bite of her Italian ice. "Okay, but let's take this conversation to go." He nodded and scooped up the last of his ice and shoved the whole spoonful into his mouth as she laughed.

Cassey loved talking about her family. Not only were they her favorite people, but they were her favorite subject as well.

As they walked along the beach, the cool salt wind hitting their faces, she told him story after story about how her brothers had convinced her of such things as the existence of aliens and ghosts, and even that the tooth fairy stole all your teeth if you didn't put your lost tooth under the pillow.

When she was small, she'd been tossed about by her brothers in the pool or when she'd gone surfing with Cole, as her brothers learned that trying new tricks was easier with a small girl. Cole usually instigated tossing her around. He practiced his surf moves with her on his shoulders until he was pleased with his moves. She would get tired of being tossed about in the waves, and he'd had to rescue her a dozen or so times when he'd pushed it past her energy limits.

Once, when she'd gotten into a fight at school with a few other girls, Marcus had taken her to his judo classes and forced her to learn some basic moves. Roman had taught her how to punch like a pro and, after a particular incident in the girls' locker room, the girls had never picked on her again.

He laughed at all of her stories as he held her hand, sending heat traveling up her arm and into her chest. She'd never really talked about her family to a man she was seeing before. Actually, some of the men she'd dated in the past had been friends of her brothers. Two of them had been best friends with Roman, who had set her up. It was funny; Roman was always trying to set her up, but had never really dated anyone that she could remember.

His brothers had always given him grief about it, but Cassey knew why he didn't date. He'd told her he'd already found the woman he wanted to grow old with, and he was just waiting for her to discover it was him she wanted to spend the rest of her life with.

As a young teenager, she'd sighed and imagined a beautiful woman who'd won her brother's heart doing some heroic deed. But the girl was blinded and couldn't see what a wonderful man she had right in front of her face. To this day, she still didn't know who that girl was or if Roman felt the same way about her still.

"So, tell me why you fought with your father tonight," she asked once they were back in his car, traveling back towards Surf Breeze.

He glanced over at her, looking a little surprised. "Actually, it was about you."

It was her turn to look surprised. "Me?"

He nodded. "Yes. My father isn't happy with the lack of progress I'm having persuading you to sell your place."

She glanced out the window and wished she hadn't asked. "I didn't mean to…"

"Hey." He took up her hand and waited until she looked back his direction. "It's okay. If it wasn't this tonight, it would have been something else. Honestly, I'm thinking of quitting."

"Quitting? Can you quit your family?"

He laughed. "I don't know, but I'm thinking of trying." She smiled at him and chuckled a little.

"I suppose you *can* quit your family. I quit my first family, my father and stepmother, when I was seven. Of course I had the help of my guardian angel."

He glanced over at her. "What?"

She smiled. "Lilly, the social worker who saved my life and brought me to the Graytons."

"You were seven?" he asked.

"Yes," she nodded, looking out the window, remembering that night so many years ago. "Until I was seven, I'd only left my house about three times. Each time, I had to hide in the truck so no one would see how bad of shape I was in. I spent most of my time locked in the cellar or in a closet because they kept catching me sneaking food. It wasn't so bad until my father married again. At least I think they were married." She closed her eyes, trying to remember, but she'd blocked a lot of her childhood memories out. "Kimberly, my stepmother, was left in charge of me a lot during the day. She liked to sit on the couch and watch television, and small children tend to make a lot of noise. So, I stayed locked in the basement from the time my father left before sunrise until he returned home after dark."

"How terrible." He flexed his fingers on hers.

She looked over at him. "Then I came to the Graytons and found my real family. I remember the first few months I felt guilty for being allowed all different kinds of food. Lilly had given me my first Coke that night." she smiled. "I guess you can say the addiction started then."

He smiled. "Well, I haven't even met the

Graytons and I like them already."

"You would. They would like you as well. They are always looking to take in people like us." She realized what she'd said too late.

"People like us?" he asked.

She nodded a little. "I guess so. You know…" She shrugged her shoulders and looked out the window. "My parents may have abused me physically, but from the sound of it, yours have neglected you. Neglect is a form of abuse, too."

He thought about it. "I suppose you're right. Funny, I think I could have handled it a lot better had they tossed me around a little. You know, my father never really yelled at me until after Calvin was gone."

"He probably misses him a lot. I can't imagine what it's like losing someone so close to you."

"You can't? From what you said, your sister took off at seventeen and hasn't been back. Isn't that a lot like losing her?"

She thought about it and then shook her head. "No. I know Marissa is out there somewhere. She chose to leave us; Calvin didn't get a choice."

"I suppose you're right. But I would think it would hurt just the same. The emptiness, the place they used to fill." He squeezed her hand a little. "Have you ever thought about looking for her?"

She shrugged her shoulders and looked out the window. It was too dark to see anything, but she'd driving this road enough to know what was out there. Trees, homes, an occasional glimpse of the shoreline. Marissa was out there somewhere, probably close enough to reach out and touch if she'd tried.

"I looked once, shortly after she left," she whispered.

"And?"

"She doesn't want to be found. If she did, she would have left some clues for me."

"What kind of clues?"

She turned and looked at him. "Why are you so interested?"

He shrugged his shoulder and dropped her hand to maneuver around a sharp turn. "It's a mystery." He smiled at her when the road straightened out. "I like solving mysteries."

She tilted her head a little, looking at him across the dark car. "We always talked about what we wanted to do when we grew up. I was determined from the tender age of eleven to open my own bar and grill." She chuckled. "Marissa had other ideas. She wanted to buy old houses and fix them up. She was always helping Marcus and Roman out when they worked around the house we grew up in. The three of them made a really great team. She kept stacks of newspaper clippings in a box; she'd cut home listings out and dream about fixing the places up. After she left, I drove by every house she'd ever looked at." The sadness still overwhelmed her sometimes. "She always talked about a place overlooking Dolphin Bay, being close to Spring Haven. I know she's somewhere close, but until she wants to be found, she is going to stay hidden."

"Any idea why she left?"

"Yes and no. I know it had nothing to do with me or the Graytons. She had a big fight with Roman the day before she left, but I don't think it had anything to do with that, either. She'd started going out with some boy. Tommy, I think, was his name. Roman didn't like Tommy. He thought he was bad news, and he was right. I didn't even like the guy. That last night, when we talked, I told her my thoughts. She sounded so sad, like I'd hurt her somehow." She hadn't realized she was crying, until a tear slipped down her cheek. She wiped it away quickly, before Luke could see it. Turning her head back towards the window, she shrugged. "Her note said she wanted to discover who she was on her own. That she loved us all and that we shouldn't worry."

"It sounds like she just wanted her independence. Maybe she's living her dream?"

"She was always worrying that she was going to turn out like her mother. Her mother had gotten pregnant with her in her teens. She drank and did drugs and never really took care of Marissa. She thought that the condition was hereditary. I asked her whether, if her condition, as she liked to call it, was hereditary, I was destined to have a kid and lock them away. She said, no, because it was my father who had done that to me." Cassey shook her head. "She claimed that the bad genes were passed on from mother to daughter, and that I had lucked out because my mother had died when I was young, so I didn't know how I would turn out. We were so naive."

He chuckled. "Kids think all sorts of things. I thought that my father was the smartest man on earth."

They drove up and parked next to her back door. She looked at the back of her place and sighed. "I just wish Marissa was here, so she could see that I've fulfilled my dream."

He reached over and took her hand. "She'd be proud of what you've built for yourself here."

Cassey smiled and nodded. It was too hard to say anything since there was a lump in her throat just thinking about it. She'd never talked to anyone about Marissa like this before, even her brothers. She wondered why she had chosen Luke to open up to about it all.

Chapter Nine

The next few days, Luke spent as much time as he could with Cassey. His father kept calling him on his cell, and each time he would put him off. He'd spent most nights in her bed, so he'd canceled his hotel reservation. He thoroughly enjoyed the time he spent with her and wondered how much longer it was all going to last. He knew he couldn't put his father off much longer.

He worked on his laptop during the day while Cassey worked. It wasn't that he had a lot of stuff to do for Crystal Shores. To be honest, his father had put him in charge of meaningless tasks, and he was beginning to feel more like a secretary than a son and the heir to the empire.

It was hard looking at everything Cassey had done for herself and comparing it to his life. Sure,

133

he had a business degree where she just had some night school. But she was actually building her own empire instead of mooching off of her family. The more he thought about it, the more he wanted to get out from under his family's control.

He'd actually started taking measures to secure his own future in the last few days. He'd been spending more time working on his own business plan than working for his father. And he didn't care what the consequences were.

He was punching away at his laptop and didn't realize someone had come into the office until he cleared his throat behind him. Looking around, he saw a man in his twenties with dark hair and deep blue eyes glaring at him. He tensed.

"Just who the hell are you and what are you doing in my sister's place?"

Luke relaxed a little. "You must be Marcus." He stood and held out his hand. "I'm Luke Callaway." He waited for the man to shake his hand, but he just continued to stand there looking at him.

"Callaway? Crystal Shores Callaway?" Luke nodded. "You've answered one of my two questions."

Luke laughed a little. "I'm staying here for a while, with your sister."

"Well, why didn't you say so?" The man took his hand and shook it. A smile crossed his face and Luke had an instant liking for him.

"Cass didn't mention you." He grabbed the chair next to Luke's, turned it backwards, and straddled it, crossing his arms over the back. "I just left her downstairs. She told me she'd bring me up some lunch. Maybe you'll get lucky and get some, too." Marcus smiled.

Luke looked at the clock on his computer and sat back down. "Yeah, she usually brings it up around now. Cassey tells me you're in the building business."

Marcus nodded. "Homes, businesses, you name it. You in the market for a building?"

"Might be. I've been working on a business plan and have my eye on a property on the outskirts of town."

Marcus' eyebrows shot up. "The fifteen acres on Mercer Street?"

Luke nodded and smiled. "Sound like a good lot?"

Marcus nodded. "Been thinking about what could go there for years. Would make a great place for a hotel. Is Crystal Shores looking at expanding to Surf Breeze?"

Luke shook his head, but before he could answer, Cassey walked in with three Styrofoam boxes stacked on each other.

They sat around the table and chatted while they ate. Marcus kept his mouth quiet about Luke's plans, and Luke liked him even more for it. After

Cassey left to head back downstairs, they finished their conversation. Luke told Marcus his plans and asked that he keep them quiet for now, at least until the ink was dry on the contracts. They shook hands and Luke knew he had taken his first step towards releasing his father's hold on his life. Now all he had to do was head to the bank or someplace worse—his grandfather's place.

Cassey watched Luke walking towards her. She'd enjoyed the lunch with him and Marcus, and she thought her brother approved of Luke. Not that it meant much; Marcus usually approved of anyone she dated. It was Roman that any man she dated had to get past.

Luke was wearing a suit and tie, and every woman in the place watched him walk across the floor. When he stepped up to her and kissed her on the lips, she thought she heard a few sighs.

"You clean up pretty well." She smiled and wrapped her arms around his shoulders.

"I've got a meeting. Shouldn't take too long. If all goes well, I'd like to celebrate with dinner tonight."

She nodded and smiled. She watched him walk away and sighed herself. He sure did make a wonderful sight in his suit.

An hour later, she was shocked to see Luke's father walk through her front doors. He made a beeline towards her after he spotted her standing across the room. She excused herself from the couple she was talking to and met him across the floor.

"Miss Grayton." He nodded. "Do you have someplace we can talk?"

She nodded and took him to her office. She motioned for him to sit in the chair in front of her desk. He remained standing, so she sat behind her desk, shoving her hands under her desk so he wouldn't notice how much they shook. What was he doing here?

"I understand my son has been staying here." He looked down at her, disgust written all over his face.

Instead of saying anything, she nodded her head in agreement.

"Typical," he said harshly. "I send him down here to do a job, and he decides to take a vacation and sleep around while he's at it." He turned and started to pace in her small office. "What will it cost me this time?" he said after he turned and glared at her again.

"I'm sorry?" she asked, shocked.

"Come now, Miss Grayton, everyone has their price. I need you to break it off quickly with him. Today, if possible. I understand you're not in the market to sell your...little place here. I'm willing to overlook that, but I won't have you dragging my son's name through the mud, so to speak."

The shaking in her hands stopped; instead, she started to grind her back teeth. Slowly placing her hands on her desk, she rose up to her full height. "I don't know who you think you are, but I can't be bought off. You have—"

"I'm a concerned father," he broke in as he walked to the front of her desk. "I'll give you this chance. You won't get another," he warned.

"I don't need another. As far as I'm concerned, you can get out now." She leaned slightly on her desk, watching his dark eyes grow fierce.

"Fine," he said, staring at her. "There are other methods for getting what I want. I will have this place, or see it closed down, just to prove my point." He turned and started to walk out.

When the door shut behind him, she sat back down as the shaking started up again. When Luke walked back in an hour later, she was still sitting there, a plan forming in her mind.

"Hey," he said, smiling.

"Hi." She motioned for him to sit down. Was it really only two weeks ago that she'd met him for the first time in this very room? How had she let herself be drawn into his life, his mess, so quickly? "Luke, I think we need to talk." She waited until the smile fell away from his face. "Let's be honest, we both knew this wasn't going to work out. It's not as if we walked into this with any assumptions."

He nodded and crossed his arms over his chest. "What led you down this path?"

She shook her head. "I'm not the kind of person to get close to. I've never had a relationship past a few weeks. Which is one of the reasons I was honest with you from the beginning."

He nodded. "You were." He stood and leaned on the front of her desk. "What brought this on now? Did you get a visit from my father?"

She nodded. "But my decision has nothing to do with his visit. I asked him to leave and he threatened the bar and grill."

"I'm sure he did." He leaned up and looked down at her. "I wouldn't take his threats lightly."

She nodded. "From what I heard, he cares about you."

He laughed. "Right. You don't have to do this. I can help you. I can help your bar and grill."

She shook her head. "I don't need your help." She stood. "I hope we can remain—"

"Don't." He walked around the desk and pulled her close, crushing her hands next to his chest. As he dipped his head down, she heard him moan. His lips crushed hers as she grabbed hold of his suit jacket. She could feel the anger and frustration slowly leave him as his mouth heated hers, leaving more than her hands shaking.

When he pulled away, he looked down at her. "Don't say we can still be friends. It wouldn't work. I want you still, and I can't imagine a time in the future when I won't want you. I want much more than just friendship." He turned and walked out the door without another word.

She slid down to her chair, her spine melted to the back. She'd never been kissed like that before, and she hoped to God she would never be kissed like that again by anyone else. Closing her eyes, she let the tears slide down her cheeks.

Two hours later, after showering and dressing, she walked downstairs and went to work. The kitchen was understaffed tonight, thanks to the flu that was going around, so she spent her time back there, helping out. By the end of the night, she was exhausted and fell into bed fully dressed.

That next week, it only got worse as more and more of her staff called in sick. She worked the bar, waited and bussed tables, and even did dishes. She didn't mind since keeping busy was helping her keep her mind off of Luke. When she fell into bed each night, she missed feeling him next to her. She missed talking to him as she ate her lunch in the courtyard, so she started eating lunch in her office. When that didn't work, she sat in the dining room or at the bar.

As more time went by, she realized she couldn't fool herself. She'd fallen for Luke and it frustrated her to realize it. Now she just needed to decide what she was going to do about it.

The next day, she forgot completely about Luke when she found a large sign taped over her doors stating that the Health Department had closed the building until further notice.

She stood in line for two hours at the local county building to meet with the head of the health department. After arguing with him about his schedule and how much money she would lose if he didn't come out soon, she finally convinced him to come out in the next forty-eight hours.

When she walked away from the building, she was still unclear what had caused them to close her doors in the first place. He'd mentioned something about violations but had yet to present her with a list or any explanations. The worst part was that Boardwalk Bar and Grill would be closed over the weekend, her busiest days. She thought she knew who was responsible.

When she walked down the boardwalk, she noticed three more signs posted on doors and felt her frustration grow. Instead of walking to the bar and grill, she marched to her car and the steam didn't stop rolling off her until she parked in front of Crystal Shores. Before she knew what she was doing, she was standing outside Luke's father's office, listening to his secretary tell her that he wasn't available. She marched around the woman's desk and opened one of the double doors.

141

When she barged in, she noticed two things: one, he wasn't alone, and two, his face was beet red as he yelled at his son.

Luke sat in a leather chair, looking rather smug as his father stuttered over him.

"What the hell?" He turned and glared at her. "Carolyn, get in here."

His secretary was right on her heels and quickly apologized as Cassey walked forward, more determined than ever.

"Mr. Callaway, I understand your beef with me, but those other shops had nothing to do with me. For you to shut them down as well is low." She stopped right in front of him, her back and shoulders rod straight as she crossed her arms over her chest.

"Leave us, Carolyn," he barked and then waited until the woman shut the door gently with a quiet click. "I'm sure, Miss Grayton, I don't know what it is you are talking about." He walked behind his desk and sat down. Just the way he said her name made her back teeth grind.

"You may have friends in high places and be able to shut me down for the weekend, but Alfred, Marvin, and Judy had nothing to do with our little disagreement."

He waited, just looking at her. Luke stood up. "What's all this about?" he asked, concern lacing his voice.

She turned on him. "As if you didn't already know. You warned me this might happen. I suppose I should have paid more attention. He had the health department shut down all the food venders along the boardwalk. No food equals no business for any of us. People are going to stop coming to Surf Breeze altogether. I can't believe the city agreed to your scheme." She turned back to Mr. Callaway who was now looking quite smug behind his desk.

"Is this true, Dad?" Luke asked. When his father didn't answer, he picked up an envelope his father had been waving around when she walked in and tossed it at him. "I'm done. No more arguments, no more conversations. You won't even see me for the holidays." He grabbed her hand and started walking out the door. When they made it into the hallway, she yanked her hand away and turned on him.

"Don't tell me you didn't know his plans." The anger still radiated through her. Her rational mind screamed at her to stop, but she was working on adrenaline now.

"Cassey, I didn't know what he was up to. I swear it. I haven't seen him or talked to him since the night we ate dinner a few weeks ago." He held out his hands and took a step back.

She looked at him, gauging his face, and could see he was telling the truth. After a minute, she sighed and relaxed her shoulders. "I'm sorry; it's been an emotional day."

"I understand. Have you eaten lunch?"

She was so caught up in her anger towards his father, it took a moment for her to process what he had asked her.

Chapter Ten

Cassey sat across from him at his favorite fast food place in town, and he could see the wariness in her face. Her silver eyes, which were normally bright, were dull and foggy looking. There were purple blotches under those eyes, and he could tell she wasn't getting enough sleep. She looked like she'd lost some weight as well, but he knew better than to mention it.

He reached across the table and touched her hand lightly. "Has it been that bad?"

"What?" She looked up at him as she rubbed her forehead. "No." He could tell she had just automatically denied it.

When he sighed and looked at her, she closed her eyes and lowered her hand from her temple.

"Yes, okay, it has. Half of my staff has been out the last few weeks with the flu." She laughed a little. "To be honest, at first I thought that was your father's doing. Then this morning, after seeing the notice, I spent a few hours arguing with the local health inspector, who is apparently the *only* health inspector in Adams County. After going back and forth, I finally got him to agree to come back down to my place and reinspect on Monday afternoon. When I walked back from the meeting, I noticed that two other places, including The Lunch Box, were closed down due to violations as well. I can't even remember driving to Emerald Beach." She closed her eyes and shook her head.

"I'm sorry you're having to deal with all this by yourself," he said and meant it. He wished she hadn't turned him away. It had hurt not being with her, but the time apart had only reinforced his desire to be with her. He'd taken so many steps in the last few days, and he knew that once he had everything lined up, he would find a way to change her mind about their relationship. All he needed was some time.

"It's not that bad. I have the new inspection on Monday." She shrugged her shoulders. "I've given the employees a day off."

"A day?" he asked, his curiosity in his voice.

"Yes, everyone is scheduled to be in first thing Sunday for a complete cleaning of the place. I want that inspector to be able to eat off the floor." She smiled and he gained even more respect for her.

"I've got nothing to do on Sunday if you need another set of hands." Her smiled dropped away a little, and he could see concern flash in her eyes.

"I don't know." She looked off, pulling her hand away. She shook her head and looked back at him. "I just don't think I can deal with you right now."

He felt like laughing. "Deal with me?"

She nodded. "You—" She stopped and swallowed, and then reached for her iced tea and took a sip. "You said you couldn't be friends with me."

He waited, taking a breath before he spoke. "No, I said I want to be more than just friends, and I still mean it."

She looked off over his shoulder. He could see her eyes water up a little as her hand went to her forehead again and started rubbing her temple.

"I can't." She shook her head lightly.

"Can't or just don't want to?"

She blinked, holding her eyes closed for a moment. "Both. I have too much to handle right now. I don't think I can deal with trying to figure out what is going on between us."

He thought about it. "What if we went back to how it was before?"

147

She blinked and looked at him. "How?"

He smiled a little, deciding that it might just work. Reaching across the table, he picked up her hand and leaned a little closer. "Cassey, I want you…physically. I know you want me, too." He watched heat replace the weariness in her eyes. "This way, I can be there to help you out. I want to be there for you."

"I…" She sighed and he could see her mind changing. "I just don't know." He had to do something quick, or he'd lose his chance, lose her. He didn't want to lose her.

"What do you say I drive you home? I've been staying in Surf Breeze for almost a week now."

"What about your car? Didn't you drive here?"

He shook his head. "My father sent a car for me. I really had no choice but to come." She looked at him for the first time. He was wearing a ratty shirt and sweats—not his normal clothing.

"What did he do," she chuckled, "send the hulk after you?"

He looked down and realized his gym clothes had gotten a few more holes in them since the last time he'd worn them. Laughing, he nodded. "Ricardo can seem like it sometimes. Think of your Tyrone on steroids."

She whistled. "Why does your father employ someone like that?" She leaned forward, taking another sip of her tea. For the first time today, her eyes actually sparkled.

"Oh, you'd be surprised who my father has threatened before." He stood up, gathering their tray and trash. "What do you say I tell you all about it as I drive you home?"

She sighed and leaned back. "Fine, you win. I'm too tired to argue or drive back by myself." She stood and waited until he'd cleared their table. "You know…" She smiled as they walked out the door. "I could use a new bus boy." He laughed.

He talked to her as they drove back to Surf Breeze, telling her stories of his childhood and of what he'd heard about his father from some of the people who'd worked for him over the years. She'd listened and laughed, but he'd kept the stories lighthearted and upbeat. There was no reason to mention some of the more aggressive moves his father and grandfather had made in the name of keeping the family business thriving.

By the time they pulled into the parking lot next to her apartment, her eyes were barely open. He brushed a strand of hair over her shoulder.

"You look beat." He smiled a little.

"I feel beat. Listen, I'm probably not going to make the best company."

He shook his head and pulled her as close as he could with the middle console in the way. "Cassey, you don't have to always entertain me. I've got my laptop." He nodded towards the dark bag in her back seat. "And I have some work that I can do."

She sighed and rested her head on his shoulder. "How about some hot chocolate and an old movie instead?"

He smiled. "Sounds wonderful."

An hour later, his left arm was completely numb behind her neck as she slept peacefully against his shoulder. *The Towering Inferno* played quietly on the set. He'd turned the volume almost all the way down when he'd seen her eyes close for the fourth time. Their hot chocolate mugs sat on the coffee table, empty. He'd made a large bowl of microwave caramel popcorn, which she had barely touched.

He knew she was under a lot of stress, thanks to his father. Actually, he was sure that in the next few weeks, he was going to be dealing with some of his own problems because of his family.

He wanted to finish some of the work he'd hoped to complete today before being whisked away by his father.

Shifting, he pulled Cassey close and easily carried her into her room. She moaned a little then snuggled closer to him as he walked sideways through her bedroom door. Laying her down gently on her bed, he watched as she snuggled into her soft pillow. He pulled off her low heels and smiled at her bright pink toenails. He'd missed that about her in the last few weeks; her toes were the cutest he'd ever seen. Her ankles weren't half-bad either. He smiled as his eyes followed her long limbs up her body. She was a nice package, he thought, as his eyes rested on her eyelashes. He frowned a little when he noticed the dark circles under her eyes.

Walking into the next room, he pulled out his laptop and got to work, trying to counter anything he thought his father would throw at him in the next few weeks.

By midnight, he thought he had all his bases covered. He'd emailed all the contractors he'd been working with as well as his contact down at the city office to confirm his permits wouldn't be disturbed. He had even composed a press release, which he'd sent to several local papers along the coast. He thought that once word was out about his new business, there would be no stopping him.

He stood up, stretched his hands over his head, and rolled his neck. He was a little stiff, since his workout had been cut short by his father and he hadn't been able to cool down. Walking down the hallway, he pulled off his tennis shoes and climbed into the bed. Cassey rolled over in sleep and snuggled up against his side. He wrapped his arm around her and closed his eyes. For the first time in weeks, he felt at peace.

Cassey was back at her old house, looking around in the dark room. She held her breath as someone walked by. She prayed that it was her father but could tell by the way the floorboards creaked from the extra weight that it was Kimberly. Out of the two of them, Kimberly was worse. Her father usually only got mad at her when he was tired or hungry, but Kimberly was mad all the time.

There wasn't enough light in the little room to see anything, so when the door opened and light flooded in, she closed her eyes to the blinding brightness. Her heart beat in her ears, deafening her to everything so she was now both blind and deaf to what was going to happen next. Her arm was yanked hard as she was pulled up off the floor. Her tiny arm popped as she was pulled from the closet area, and as she tried to stand, her legs folded underneath her because she'd been sitting for too long.

No words were spoken as the large hands tried to get her to walk, pushing her forward. She stumbled as her legs started working. Her eyes were still closed to the brightness of the room. When she fell, she landed hard on her hands and knees and as her eyes flew open, she screamed.

"Cassey!" Luke shook her over and over and finally her eyes opened. "It's just a dream." He gathered her close as her heart beat frantically in her chest. Her hands shook as she wrapped her arms around his shoulders.

The dreams always returned when she was stressed. She should have expected the nightmare after what had transpired yesterday. She knew what had come after her eyes opened, how close that particular beating had come to ending her. It had taken days before she'd been able to open her jaw and months before she could walk again.

When her father had gotten home, Kimberly had told him that she'd tried to call the police on them. She didn't even know how to use a phone, let alone how to call anyone for help. But her father had just made a spot for her to lie down in the basement, and that had become her new prison until she'd finally escaped that fateful night.

"I'm okay now," she said into his chest. When he pulled back and looked at her, she realized the light on his side of the bed was on. She wondered how long it had taken him to wake her. Back when she was living at home, it sometimes took all three of her brothers to get her eyes to finally open and her mind to clear from the dreams.

His eyes showed his concern. "Are you sure? You were screaming so loud." He gathered her up one more time for a light hug.

Nodding her head, she closed her eyes for just a moment to enjoy the feel of him next to her. It had been too long. She'd missed how he felt, how he smelled. Then he was pulling back and sitting up, leaning against her headboard.

She sighed and followed him up. "I know you

want to know what that's all about." When he nodded, she rested her head back against the headboard and started rubbing her forehead. The headache that came after the dreams had already started. "I've told you how the Graytons saved my brothers, my sister, and myself. When I was seven, I ran away from my father and stepmother." She opened her eyes and looked at him.

He had relaxed a little and was patiently waiting to hear her story.

"Until I was five, they'd kept me locked me in a small closet. They only allowed me out once a day to go to the bathroom. If I had accidents, they would beat me, so I learned early to control myself. It wasn't as if they were feeding me a lot, and they only let me drink a little water as well. I must have just turned six when Kimberly, my stepmother, beat me so bad that I was confined to a cot in the basement for months. That ten by eight clearing in the basement became my new cell. I now had a dirt floor, which I could use as a bathroom any time I wanted, and enough room that I could walk and use my legs for the first time in my life. My legs got stronger, and one night, I crawled up a stack of junk in the basement and crawled out the window. I ran until I was out of energy, and then I hid under a tree. That's where my guardian angel found me." She smiled, remembering seeing Lilly for the first time. "She'd watched the house for weeks, knowing there was a child living there but never seeing me. My father kept telling them that I had died with my mother, but Lilly never gave up. I had left the house three time in my life. The third time, someone had seen me hiding in my father's truck and called social services." She smiled. "You know, the only reason I was in the truck that day was because it was my birthday. My father thought of the little trip to the gas station as a sort of birthday present. Half the time, I'd kept my eyes closed tightly, because I wasn't used to the bright lights."

"Tell me they paid for what they did to you." His voice was low, and she could see the anger in his eyes.

She nodded. "For a while, yes. When I was in high school, I overheard the Graytons talking about how they had both gotten out of jail. For years after, I was afraid they would hunt me down and make me pay. But I haven't heard from or seen them since, and I stopped worrying that they would find me."

"I can only imagine how horrible living like that must have been." He pulled her close and kissed the top of her head. "How could you recover from something like that?"

"The Graytons were the only reason I got over everything so quickly. Them and my brothers and Marissa. Hearing what each one of them had gone through helped me recover and learn to trust."

"You're amazing." He pulled back and looked down at her as she smiled up at him.

"I only have the dreams when I've had an emotional day." She frowned a little.

"I've been doing some thinking about your situation." He glanced over at the clock. "But it's too early to talk shop right now." He pulled her down until they were lying down. She moved around until he was spooning her, his mouth right by her ear. "Rest some more." He kissed her neck, just below her ear. "And this time dream of me." He kissed her gently again.

She did, and when she woke three hours later, she felt totally refreshed. It didn't hurt to have Luke's warm body next to hers. His arms were wrapped tightly around her in slumber. When she tried to move, he pulled her closer as she laughed.

"Good morning." She turned and looked into his brown eyes.

"Hmmm." He leaned in and placed a warm kiss on her lips. "Yes it is." She could feel his legs wrap around her hips as he started to run his hands over her shoulders. "Did you dream of me?"

She blushed a little, remembering how the rest of her night's dreams had gone. Seeing her blush, he smiled slowly. "Care to tell me exactly what I did to you in your dreams that would cause this?"

She giggled and then sobered. "How about I show you?" She leaned over and looked down at him as she placed a soft kiss on his lips. Her hands went to his hair, holding his mouth to hers. Straddling him, she felt his morning desire, which matched the heat that had spread throughout her body. She'd removed her clothes in the middle of the night, and now she wore a black pair of underwear shorts and a black tank top. His hands roamed over her hips as she pressed her desire to his.

She felt his hips jump as the friction between them heated up. His gray gym shorts were easy enough to pull down his hips. Removing his T-shirt, she soaked in the sight of him. It looked like he'd been working out a lot since the last time she'd seen him. His arms looked bigger; the muscles were more defined as she ran her fingers over each new one.

"Mmmm, I like." She looked up into his eyes and smiled. He flexed under her touch, and she couldn't stop herself from dipping her head to lick her way down to his navel. She took her time exploring the six-pack along the path.

When she gripped him, he moaned, closed his eyes, and said under his breath, "You're killing me."

"Now you know how I feel when you touch me." She smiled as his hips moved under her fingers. His nails dug into her shoulders, pulling her up until she was poised just above him.

"Now. My God, Cassey, now," he cried out.

As she watched his face, she slowly slid down on his full length. How had she gone almost two whole weeks without this? Without him?

When she started to move, he used his hands on her hips to push and pull her and then flipped their positions as he said, "Too slow."

When her back hit the mattress, she released a nervous giggle, then a groan as he pulled her knees up to her chest and thrust deeper, faster.

His eyes locked with hers as he pounded his hips next to hers. Their breathing became labored as a small bead of sweat formed on his temple. His hands were coarse as he reached down and gently cupped her breast. When he leaned down and placed a searing kiss on her lips, she closed her eyes and jerked her hips with her release, knowing he was close behind her.

They lay there for a few minutes until she had gained her breath back. Then he hoisted her up in his arms and carried her to the shower.

He took his time using the soap and his hands to clean her gently. She was so relaxed by the time he stepped out of the shower, leaving her to rinse herself off, that she felt like her knees were made of putty.

A few minutes later, when she finally pulled herself from the shower, she smelled food and heard him banging around in the kitchen.

She dressed in some stretchy pants and an oversized shirt, combed her hair, and applied a small amount of makeup. When she walked out onto the patio, she saw him punching away on his laptop. There were two covered plates sitting on the table next to him. When he looked up, she smiled at him.

"You didn't have to make breakfast." She sat down and uncovered the plate. A large heap of French toast and scrambled eggs sat on the plate. "Wow, this must be your plate." She went to move it towards him.

"No. I can't seem to cook just a little. I guess it's a learned thing. When I start making French toast, I usually make the whole loaf of bread." He chuckled.

"Well, if I eat all this, you're going to have to roll me around today." She laughed and ate a forkful of food. The French toast was perfect. The crust was a little crunchy and he'd added a hint of cinnamon and something else she couldn't quite put her finger on.

"Peanut butter," he said, smiling over at her.

"Hmmm?" She looked up at him in question.

"The secret ingredient is peanut butter." He nodded towards the French toast and smiled.

"You put peanut butter in French toast?" She looked down at her plate in astonishment.

He nodded. "Actually, you spread just a little over it when it's hot. You know, instead of butter. That way when you pour the syrup over it, it all melts and give you that little extra taste."

"Wow." She took another bite. "My new favorite way to eat French toast." She smiled up at him and a little part of her melted.

Chapter Eleven

Luke stood across from Cassey and tried not to look at her for the millionth time. Her hair was tied back with a white handkerchief. She wore a white T-shirt and an old pair of faded jeans, which looked damn sexy on her. There was a little bit of dust on her chin and he could see a bead of sweat on her brow. She was wearing large pink rubber gloves and when she bent down to clean the bottom shelf of the stove, he couldn't remove his eyes from how the jeans accented her tight bottom.

"You have it bad, bro." Marcus slapped his shoulder.

"What?" He jumped a little as he forced his eyes away from Cassey's exotic rear end.

Marcus nodded towards his sister. "You know,

161

I've never seen her so distracted before."

"Distracted?" Luke looked over to where Cassey was shoulder-deep in the large oven, her arms and gloves covered in dark stains from the dirt she was meticulously cleaning.

Marcus laughed and punched his shoulder again. "Since I've known her longer, you'll just have to trust me on this one."

Luke shook his head and tried to get back to work as Marcus continued to talk to him, telling him funny stories about when he was young.

They were standing in the large walk-in freezer, removing out-of-date produce. There was a large trash can that was almost full, but the shelves were still lined with produce that they could keep. As long as the inspector allowed Cassey to open back up, she would only lose minimal stock.

Less than ten minutes later, Marcus received a call on his cell and stepped out to answer it.

"Gotta take this," he mouthed as he walked out.

Luke turned back to the task at hand, which was organizing the frozen meat section. He wasn't much of a cook himself, but he knew that the food stocked in the small freezer was high quality. Looking down at a bucket of fish, he wondered what she would do with all of it if she was forced to close down for a while.

"That bad, huh?" Cassey asked, walking over to him, a frown on her lips as she looked into the bucket.

"Hmm?" He looked up from the large icy bucket of fish. "Oh, no, they're fine."

"Good." She smiled a little and leaned against the wall of the freezer. "Well, I've done all I can do with the stoves." She wiped her arm across her face, leaving a streak on her cheek.

He chuckled and stepped closer to her. Using a towel, he wiped the spot away. "You know, there isn't one speck of dust left in this place. I know the inspector will approve you." He smiled down at her and flicked his finger down her nose, then lightly gripped her face and dipped for a soft kiss. "Mmm, you taste like honey."

She chuckled. "Wendy brought in some of her honey cookies. I lose all control when it comes to them."

"Mmm." He dipped his head and took another sample as he backed her up a step until her back was pressed against the wall. He felt her shiver and gasp as her back hit the cold wall. Chuckling a little, he reversed their positions until he felt the cold between his shoulder blades.

She smiled up at him and pushed against his shoulders a little more. "Cold?"

He shook his head and chuckled. "With you pressed against me, it's a wonder everything isn't melting."

She wrapped her arms around his neck and

163

reached up on her toes and started kissing him again. When she pulled away, he was beginning to wonder how the small room wasn't filled with steam.

"Cassey, let's call lunch and send everyone home," he said as he nibbled on the skin just below her ear.

She chuckled and shook her head. "Can't." She pulled back. "We have the dining room to clean after lunch."

"Fine, but at least we can give everyone a very long lunch break," he said, pulling her closer.

"Mmm, that sounds—"

"Hey, did you know that your brother is a complete idiot?" Marcus said, walking in and shaking his head.

Cassey sighed and took a step back from Luke. "I've known that for years, but you shouldn't be so hard on yourself." She smiled and punched Marcus' arm lightly.

He chuckled. "Funny. I was talking about Cole. He's heading to Australia. There's an approaching cyclone off the North Queensland coast, and he's heading to Byron Bay to surf in the massive waves they are getting." He shook his head and frowned a little.

"Cole knows what he's doing." Cassey smiled and patted her brother's shoulder. "Besides, he's really good at it."

164

"I've seen some of the footage from the storm down there." He shook his head again.

Just then, Wendy walked in. "Hey, boss, we're going to break for lunch. Do you want us to pick anything up for you?"

"No." She looked over at Luke and tried to hide the smile. "We're set."

"Where are you going?" Marcus asked, starting to walk with her. "I might head out with you."

"We're heading to—"

Luke didn't hear the rest, since Cassey was shoving him out the door and down the hallway.

"You must be starved." He chuckled when she shoved him through a doorway.

"Famished." She shut the door behind her. Since the lights were off and the door closed, he had no clue where they were. When her hands came to his chest, pushing him back against the wall, he realized he no longer cared.

Cassey couldn't seem to control the shaking. Her fingers shook as she pulled Luke's shirt off his arms. When she felt his skin exposed, she dipped her head down and licked his salty skin. He tasted better than the honey cookies she'd devoured less than a half hour ago.

His fingers went into her hair, holding her to his skin as he moaned her name over and over.

"I want you so bad," he groaned as she lapped at his flat nipples with her tongue. When her fingers reached for his belt buckle, he pushed them aside and reversed their positions until she was pushed up against the wall, her hands held over her head in one of his.

"My turn," he moaned as he flipped up her shirt and exposed her skin. With his free hand, he pushed down her bra until her nipples puckered in the cool air of the broom closet. She'd been so blinded with lust, she had settled for the first room that wasn't below zero. Now as he tugged at the hem of her jeans, she wished they were in her room and that they had the whole day to explore each other.

His hands released hers above her head and traveled down her body, exploring and causing her skin to heat where he touched. He pulled on her jeans until she was exposed, then he ran his fingers over her cotton underwear.

"Nice," he said as he played over the soft material until she felt them turn moist from her desire.

"Luke." She dug her nails into his skin, trying to pull him closer to her.

"I know," he groaned as he yanked her jeans off her long legs. Then he dug his fingers into her hips as he ran his mouth over her exposed chest. She reached for him and flipped open his jeans, then wrapped her fingers around his length. He was perfect. She could spend hours exploring the length of him, enjoying the way he felt in her hands.

His jeans hung on his hips and he almost fell when he moved to step closer to her.

Cursing under his breath, he stepped back, kicked off his shoes, and freed his legs from the jeans.

It was too dark in the small room to see clearly. She quickly disposed of the rest of her clothing when she heard him remove his. Then he came back to her and pressed up against her, starting a kiss that deepened more than any she'd ever experienced before.

He took her left leg in his hand and pulled it up high until her knee was next to his chest, fully exposing all of her to him, and then he slid into her heat as they both moaned. Her leg wrapped around his hip, pulling him closer as he pushed her back up against the wall.

"Cass, I can't..." he moaned breathlessly.

She dug her nails into his shoulders as his thrusts grew faster and harder. Her head fell back and her eyes closed to the wonder of it all. Their skin was slick with heat as the darkness veiled them, causing the feeling, tastes, and sounds to be heightened. She'd never experienced sensory overload until that moment.

His fingers traveled over her skin, pinching her nipples lightly. His lips ran over her neck, just below her ears, as he nibbled his way back to her earlobe.

When she felt herself losing control, she reached up and took his hair into her hands and pulled his mouth back to hers as she felt his final thrust.

A few minutes later, when she flipped on the light in the small closet, she tried not to laugh. It looked like a scene from a movie. Their clothes were thrown all over the small room. She found her underwear on the top shelf with several rolls of toilet paper. Her left shoe was in the empty mop bucket and her other one was wedged behind a broom.

"I didn't know you could have so much fun in a broom closet." He chuckled as he pulled on his shirt.

She smiled. "Neither did I. Maybe we should try out the supply closet upstairs sometime," she said, pulling on her shoes while trying not to fall flat on her face.

He chuckled. "I'm game."

Just then, they heard voices down the hall and stopped moving. She held her breath as she heard Wendy talking to someone outside the doorway. Screaming was more like it.

"Are you stupid?" they heard her saying. "Or do you just want to get yourself killed?"

"Neither," Cassey heard her brother Cole say. She didn't know he was still there. After what Marcus had said, she'd expected Cole to be on a plane heading to Australia.

She put her finger over her lips and nodded to Luke, who was sitting on an overturned bucket, putting on his shoes.

"I thought you'd learned your lesson last time. I won't cover for you again like that," Wendy said.

"And I appreciate your help keeping my family from finding out, but I can handle this. Besides, I need the money to help Cass out."

"Bullshit," Wendy said. "You live for the danger. It's a death wish."

Cole chuckled. "I told you, it's more dangerous coming around here all the time, eating those honey cookies of yours. A guy's likely to get fat and lazy sticking in the same place for too long."

"Then go," Wendy yelled. "See if I care." They heard her walk off.

"Wendy." They heard Cole chase after her.

"I didn't know they were a couple," Luke said, standing up again.

Cassey spun around quickly. "What?" Then she laughed. "No, Cole and Wendy aren't dating." She almost felt like laughing again, but something held her back. The conversation they'd just overheard could have easily been interpreted as an argument between a couple, but she knew better. Her brother had a different woman on every beach he surfed.

"Really?" He smiled at her and started walking towards her. "They could have fooled me."

She shook her head. "They fight more than my brothers do. Honestly, I don't think Wendy can stand Cole. They tolerate each other for my sake. It's a hate, hate relationship." She smiled and wrapped her arms around his neck.

"Like we used to have?" He smiled, then dipped his head down and placed a soft kiss on her lips.

Luke's words played over and over in her mind for the rest of the day. She tried to concentrate on cleaning, but she just couldn't shake what had happened during lunch.

She'd always been able to keep her feelings separate from her physical relationships. She'd always had a plan as far as relationships went. Keeping her heart safe had been the number one goal in her life. Why, then, was she starting to feel like her heart wasn't listening to the goals she'd set for herself?

Luke was the son of her enemy, or so she kept telling herself. So far, he'd been there for her, physically and personally, but he just wasn't the kind of man she saw herself falling for. For one, he was rich. She wasn't a snob but she was realistic. He'd grown up with money, lots of money. He'd probably never experienced wanting for anything in his childhood. In all the stories he'd told her about his childhood, he'd never had to go long without getting what he wanted.

He'd lived in one of the nicest hotels, eaten at one of the most expensive restaurants, and gone to school at one of the most prestigious colleges around.

By the time everyone called it an evening, she'd talked herself out of having any feelings for Luke. It was for the best. He was out of her league.

When she locked up for the night, she took a second look around. First thing in the morning, the inspector would be there, deciding her fate.

The place had never looked as clean as it did now. Everything shined. Her brothers had helped her employees for most of the day, but after lunch, Cole had left to head to the airport and his surf trip. The news had gotten wind that he'd be surfing the storm waves and it was all over the television set by nightfall.

She hadn't worried much until she stopped below one of the sets in the bar that was playing a piece about the storm, and she got her first real look at the waves her brother was flying halfway across the world to surf. Marcus walked up behind her and placed his hands on her shoulders and whispered, "He'll be fine."

Still, she wished she would have said something

else to Cole before he'd left. Maybe if she had yelled at him like Wendy had, he would have stayed.

She was standing at the top of the stairs, her hand on the railing, when Luke walked up the stairs towards her.

"Don't worry. Everything is going to go smoothly tomorrow." He smiled and took her hips into his hands.

She shook her head. "Actually, I was worrying about my brother."

He tilted his head. "Cole?" When she nodded, he smiled. "That man is an ledgend. I've never seen a surfer who was born for the water like him, and I've seen some of the best. When I was in college, I took a summer off and went to Hawaii. Spent a few months bumming around the beaches, trying to find out what I wanted to do in life. Since I can't surf, and I wasn't a threat to the locals, I made friends easily." He continued his story as he took her hand and walked the rest of the staircase towards her apartment. "Well, I bumped into Maka one day." He stopped and she watched as a smile crossed his face, reaching all the way to his eyes.

"Maka? You mean—"

He nodded. "The best surfer ever. He holds more records in surfing than they have for surfing. Well, Maka decided to take me under his wing that summer." He paused as she opened her door. "He told me that if I wanted to, I could be surfing like him by the end of the summer." He shook his head. "I sat with him on the beach, and every day he would try to convince me to get in the water." She turned just in time to see a sad look cross his face. Reaching over, she took his arm. He shook his head and sighed. "But because of what happened to Calvin..." He shook his head again. "Anyway, I watched surfers come and go, all trying to impress Maka, seeing if they could convince him to teach them. Maka would sit and point out what each surfer was doing wrong. Then your brother showed up with a group of surfers. He wasn't there to impress the great Maka. Instead, he headed down the beach to a spot where the surfing wasn't as good and enjoyed the water. Maka saw him down the way surfing and took my arm and said, "There, that one. He has a ka'i'ininokekai, water heart. He has the power to ride whatever wave he wants in life. Look how he stands, how he rides the waves like they are made just for him."

"He said that about Cole?" She reached for his arm. Luke nodded.

"I left the next day after my father tracked me down and told me he'd signed me up for summer classes." He shook his head. "Cole will be fine. He was the best surfer on the beach in Hawaii, and I'm sure he will be the best in Australia."

She smiled up at him. "I know you're right. Now all I have to worry about is the inspector tomorrow."

173

He chuckled. "I have a few ideas to keep your mind off that." He pulled her close and kissed her until she no longer worried about her brother or the inspector.

Chapter Twelve

Luke woke early the next morning. He could feel Cassey's hair on his chest. Her sweet smell was surrounding him, making him wish that he didn't have a million other things that he had to do that day instead of lying naked with her in bed all day.

When she started to move under his hands, he gently kissed her skin until she calmed down again. Then, as he slid into her, he heard her gasp and watched her eyes open and focus on him.

"Morning." He smiled down at her, and she smiled back, wrapping her arms around him. He could get used to this. Being here with her. Waking up next to her, inside of her.

They went slow as the sun rose, and then,

because they had taken a little too long in bed, they showered quickly. She grabbed a blueberry muffin and a Coke, rushed out of her apartment, and headed towards her office, where she had a few things to finish before the inspector was due.

He chose to sit outside and drink his coffee and nibble on his blueberry muffin over the morning paper.

He had several meetings today and planned to run back to Emerald Beach to finish that talk with his father. He hated to think that his old man was going to disinherit him, like he'd threatened to do, but he was determined to stick to his guns this time.

When he left Cassey, she was downstairs wiping the bar for the millionth time. He knew the inspector wasn't due to arrive for two more hours and wondered if she was going to make it that long, but then Wendy showed up and she seemed to relax a bit.

As he drove to his first meeting, he thought about last night. Just being with her again gave him the courage he needed to stand up to his father later that day. Imagining holding her made him realize he could get through the tough meeting.

The meeting with Marcus and the building inspector went very well, leaving him feeling even more lighthearted. On his drive towards Emerald Beach, he dialed Cassey's cell phone.

When she answered, he heard a bunch of

yelling in the background and got concerned until he realized it was cheering.

"Sounds like the meeting with the inspector went well."

She laughed. "Better than well. We are all set to open our doors tomorrow."

"That's really great." He smiled and turned his blinker on, moving over for a woman who was entirely too rushed to get somewhere. Since he'd installed the hands-free speakers a year ago, he'd always imagined he looked like a fool, talking to himself in the car as he drove along.

"Where are you?" she asked, and he could hear that she'd walked into a quiet room to talk to him.

"Heading to Emerald Beach. He's my father. I just couldn't leave things the way they were the other night."

The line was quiet for a while. "I hope things go well with your dad." He heard the sensitivity in her voice and wondered what he'd done to be blessed with knowing someone who cared so much. Even when his father was hell-bent on destroying her, she still cared that he could make it right with the man.

"Thanks."

"I know it may not help, but I think he loves you very much."

Luke didn't say anything for a while. "Thanks.

177

I might have to stay the night here. My mom is back from Paris today, and I know she'll want me to stay the night." He could just imagine her biting her bottom lip with this news. "I wish I could be there to hold you right now," he said softly.

"Me, too. I was hoping we'd celebrate tonight," she whispered.

Images of her flashed in his mind, causing him to smile. "Really? What would you be wearing?"

He heard her laugh. "I've been saving an outfit for just this occasion." Her voice got husky and lower. "A white bustier, white fishnet stockings, and you."

"Oh, God!" He held onto the steering wheel more tightly as his mind raced.

"Are you sure you want to stay there overnight?"

He couldn't answer. All the blood had left his brain and ended up in his pants. He wanted to turn the car back around and drive as fast as he could to get back to her.

"Luke?" she asked, giggling.

"My God, I want you so bad right now." He wished he could close his eyes and imagine her in the outfit, but the traffic was getting worse on the two-lane highway and he was just getting into town, where it looked like it was another busy weekend full of tourists.

"I want you, too. Tomorrow." He heard her

talking to someone else. "Listen, I have to go. Cole's been in an accident. I'll talk to you later." She hung up and he immediately started worrying.

He was still a few minutes out of town, so he started flipping through the radio channels, trying to find something on the news. As he drove into the parking lot at Emerald Beach, he finally found a channel that reported that surfer Cole Grayton had been injured in a motorcycle accident outside of Pensacola as he was on his way to the airport. They listed his condition as fair, but didn't have any more details.

When he walked into the building, he was so preoccupied by the news of Cole's accident that he almost walked right by his mother and a couple of women standing in the entryway.

"Oh, there you are Luke." His mother rushed over to him and hugged him lightly. His mother had always been elegant. She wore the latest fashions, stayed fit by playing tennis, and always had enough diamonds on to warrant a security guard.

"Hello, Mother." He kissed her cheek.

"You remember Jenna Wallace and her daughter Angela. I was just telling them that you should be here any minute now. They were just down for a weekend visit from New York." His mother took his arm in a vice grip and walked him towards the two women. Both of them were tall and blonde and could have been on the cover of a magazine.

179

They looked like sisters instead of mother and daughter. He could see the slight difference in age when they approached. He could also tell that Jenna had had multiple surgeries to look as young as her daughter did naturally. But it didn't negate the fact that they were both stunning women.

Upon seeing them standing in the lobby, he instantly knew his father's next step. He'd dated Angela for a few months back before Calvin had died. The relationship had been a purely physically one, and they'd left it on good terms. But looking into Angela's eyes now, he could tell that she had new motives. Thanks to his parents, most likely.

By the time he made it up to his office so he could check to see if there was any more news about Cole, he had a full-blown headache. Angela was a sensible woman, but her mother was quite the talker.

When he walked into his office, he was shocked to see it completely empty. His desk, his chairs, even his diplomas were missing. He should have known that his father would take this step. Walking into the conference room a few doors down, he pulled out his laptop and started searching for more news on Cole. He didn't find much, so he texted Cassey, letting her know that if she needed anything to let him know.

He received a text back, telling him that Marcus was driving her to Pensacola to be with Cole and that she would let him know how he was once they arrived there.

After an hour of procrastinating, he packed up his laptop and headed to his father's office. He wasn't surprised to see his mother and Jenna and Angela sitting in his father's office like they belonged there. He'd hoped to finally settle things with his dad. Knowing his father was using the Wallaces as a shield made him sure that his father was on the verge of caving.

"There you are, Luke. It's about time you got here. Your mother told me you arrived over an hour ago." His father looked at him and Luke could tell he was smirking because his office was no longer there.

"Just needed to tie up some loose ends." He smiled back at his dad and sat down in the large leather chair next to his mother.

If his father wanted to play a game of cat and mouse, far be it from him to spoil it.

Cassey sat in the passenger seat of her brother's work truck and felt like biting her nails.

"Can't you drive any faster?" She leaned forward until her seat belt clicked, shoving her back into the seat.

"Wish I could, but it's a school zone." Marcus nodded towards the yellow flashing lights and the bus full of kids ahead of them. "He'll be okay.

Roman should be there soon. He'll give us a—"

His statement was interrupted by the ringing of his phone. "Here, answer it." He handed the phone to her.

"Marcus' phone."

"Cassey?" She heard Roman's voice on the other line. "I'm here. Cole is doing fine, just a broken collar bone and arm." She could hear stress in his voice.

"What is it?"

"What?" Roman asked back.

"Roman, I can hear you're not telling me something." She worried even more. If Roman was keeping something from her, she knew it was bad.

"It's nothing to do with Cole. I swear, he's sitting up flirting with all the nurses and eating Jell-O. Don't worry about him." She could hear Cole talking in the background and she relaxed a little.

"Then what?" She heard the noise level drop a little and thought that Roman had just walked out into the hallway. She could hear a lot of machines beeping.

"I think I saw Marissa."

"What?" She sat up in the seat, the seat belt biting into her shoulder. "Where? When?"

"Here, just a few minutes before I walked into Cole's room." Her brother sighed. "When I tried to follow her, I lost her in the lobby of the hospital. Cass, she looks the same."

"Oh, Roman." She sighed and sat back. It was just like last time. To date, Roman had seen Marissa a total of ten times over the last ten years.

"What? Is the kid okay?" Marcus asked from across the seat.

She covered the phone and nodded. "Cool the jets. Broken collarbone and arm. He's already flirting with the nurses." Which, if Cole's history was anything to go off of, was the best sign.

"That kid and nurses." Marcus shook his head and focused on driving.

"Roman, we'll talk about Marissa when we get there. As a family." She heard him sigh.

"Okay, but this time I know it was her."

When they arrived, they found Cole sitting up in his hospital bed, a young nurse standing over him taking his blood pressure and another checking his IV. Everyone knew it only took one nurse to do the job, so when another one walked in, they all laughed.

"Mr. Grayton needs his rest now," a nurse told them two hours later. Cassey could see that her brother was looking tired so they headed out to dinner and the hotel that Marcus had set up for them for the night.

While they sat around eating po' boys and

drinking beer, Roman brought up Marissa.

"Are we all going to just ignore the fact that I saw Marissa earlier?" He took another drink of his beer.

"No." Cassey set her drink down. "Are you positive it was her?" When he nodded, she continued. "It's just that you seem to be the only one who ever sees her."

"I don't know what to tell you. It was her. Her hair is shorter, but she looks the same." Roman closed his eyes.

Cassey could remember her sister perfectly, but she wondered if she would recognize her if she passed by her. It had been ten years. She'd changed so much over the years; Marissa was bound to have changed as well.

"I asked all the nurses. It seems that Marissa was asking after Cole, but when she found out that he was okay, she left. The front desk nurse even confirmed that she said she was his sister." He frowned. "But she gave the woman your name."

"Mine?" Cassey frowned. "Why would Marissa use my name?"

"I don't know, but it could be one reason why we haven't found her before. We never thought about her using your name before," Roman said, frowning into his beer.

After dinner, they headed to the small hotel, where she called Luke and left him a voice mail, updating him on Cole's condition.

When she finally fell asleep, she dreamed of her sister and the day she'd arrived in Spring Haven.

She woke a few hours later to her phone ringing.

"How are you holding up?" Luke asked quietly into the phone.

"I'm okay. Better now that I know that Cole is okay. How did things go with your dad?"

She heard him sigh. "They didn't. He used some old friends to distract everyone for the night. Looks like I'll be stuck here until this weekend. Are you heading back tomorrow?"

"Yes, I'll be back in time to open up for lunch. Wendy said she would handle everything, but since Cole is okay and most likely being released tomorrow, I see no reason to stay longer."

"That's good." He sighed again. After a moment of silence, he said, "Tell me about this white bustier again."

She chuckled and proceeded to have some of the steamiest phone sex she'd ever had.

When she walked into the hospital the next morning with her brothers, they stopped at the admittance desk and asked after Marissa with no luck.

When they wheeled Cole out less than an hour later, there was a line of nurses waving goodbye to him.

"What can I say?" He smiled as Roman helped him into his car. "It was worth the pain." She watched Cole cringe as he bumped his shoulder. "Almost."

Riding back to Surf Breeze, she and Marcus talked about the possibility of Marissa using her name, and why she felt like she had to hide from her family.

"Do you think that it had anything to do with the fight we had the night before?" she asked. Everyone knew about the small fight, and even though she told herself it wasn't a big fight—they'd had worse— the thought had still played in her mind over the years.

"No," Marcus shook his head. "I think there was something else going on. Maybe she just wanted to get away? Maybe her mother had something to do with it"

"Her mother? What do you mean?"

Marcus cringed. "Nothing."

"Marcus Wyatt Grayton, you're hiding something from me. For some reason, I always thought that Marissa's mother had died."

Marcus shook his head. "She showed up a few weeks before Marissa's seventeenth birthday. Scared the shit out of everyone. Looked like she'd been hit a few times and had needle marks all over her arms. But Marissa never saw her; at least we didn't think so. We called the cops and had her removed, since the restraining order was still in effect back then."

"I didn't know." Cassey looked down at her hands. The memory of her last night with Marissa played over again in her mind.

Do you believe in fate?

Fate, sure, I guess so.

I'm destined to be like my mother.

Now she wished she could travel back in time and change her answer. Anything that would have made her sister stay.

"I wish I could see her again. To tell her…"

Marcus reached over and took her hand. "Wherever Marissa is, whatever she's doing, she's making her own way for her own reasons. She was always smart—smarter than all of us put together." He smiled over at her. It was a long joke how Marissa was a straight-A student and on honor roll.

"I know. I've never doubted that she's out there somewhere doing what she wants." She sighed and leaned against the window, watching the trees go by. "I've imagined her life so many different ways. I hope she's happy. All I ever wanted for her was to be happy."

Marcus squeezed her hand. "I'm sure she is."

By the time they drove up to her place, Cassey's mind was totally focused again on opening up the bar and grill. She was happy to see that all her employees were already there and looking very eager to open the doors. She rushed upstairs to quickly change into her work clothes, and then she headed downstairs to open. By mid-afternoon, she felt that everything was back to normal.

It took a while before she felt like she could disappear into her office, and when she did, she was greeted by a large manila envelope. She tossed it on her desk and went to answer the phone, which was ringing.

"How's my favorite girl?" she heard the man she'd come to know as her father ask on the other side of the phone. Mark Grayton had been there for her since she'd arrived at his place so long ago. After his wife, Elizabeth, died almost seven years ago, Mark had been both mother and father to the five of them. And they'd never wanted for anything. Especially since their daughter Julie was like the big sister she'd always dreamed of.

"I'm doing great. Opened up shop again today."

"So I hear. That brother of yours has talked my ear off. Seems he'll be staying with me until he's back on the surf board." He chuckled. "That kid was always breaking something."

It was true. Out of all the kids, Cole was the one most likely to have something in a sling, cast, or bandage. Maybe because he was the most adventurous out of the group.

She could remember several summers where he

couldn't go into the water due to having a cast on either his arm or leg. Once, he even had a cast on both. That was the summer Marcus dared him to drive their homemade go-cart off the docks and into the lake. But still, Cole had managed to get in more hours of surfing than most of his friends. Not to mention he'd won three trophies that fall and earned several major contracts.

Marcus was always challenging her other brothers into doing crazy things. Roman was too levelheaded to fall for most of them, whereas Cole was game for anything that sounded fun and dangerous.

She smiled, remembering her childhood with her three crazy brothers. "That's good. I'm sure you'll enjoy having him around."

"Already driving his aunt crazy. Julie says she's moving out if Cole insists on listening to his music too loud again like he did when he was younger."

She smiled, remembering all the good times up at the old house.

"Well, I know you're a busy woman, but I wanted to make sure you were coming for Thanksgiving in a few weeks."

"Thanksgiving. It can't be November already." She looked at her calendar and, sure enough, it was November 7.

"You lose track of time when you stay too busy. You need a week off, and I know just the place for it," Mark said, chuckling.

"That sounds wonderful. I'll be there. I might even bring a friend." She thought of Luke and smiled. A week in the country is just what they needed.

"Well, now, that's a first. He'll be welcomed with open arms. I'll let you get back to work."

"Thanks, Dad." She hung up and wondered why she'd just promised to bring Luke to a family holiday. It was one of the most telling signs. Meeting someone's family meant you were serious. So, the question waged in her mind—were they serious?

Chapter Thirteen

By the time Luke finally had a moment with his father later that week, he'd had enough of the Wallaces. It seemed everywhere he went, there they were.

When he worked in the smaller conference room on the second floor, Jenna just happened to be walking by after her massage three doors down. When he went for an early morning swim, there Angela was, lying by the pool, pretending she didn't remember he swam every morning.

The pair had breakfast, lunch, and dinner with his mother and father, so he couldn't get a meal with them if he tried.

It took hunting his father down in a restroom to finally get a moment alone with the man.

191

"Luke." His father looked shocked to see him in the lobby's men's restroom. "I was just heading—"

"You mean hiding," Luke interrupted.

"What?" He watched his father wash his hands quickly. He leaned back on the marble countertop.

"Face it, Dad, you've been using Mom and the Wallaces as a shield. We're going to have to talk sometime." He watched his father's face as realization came.

His father dried his hands and nodded. "Quite right. Why don't you come on up to the office now."

As they rode the elevators to the top floor, he built the courage he would need to say what had to be said. His father walked into his office and walked around his desk and sat down.

"Carolyn, hold all my calls," he barked into his phone and then turned to Luke. "Okay, what's all this about you buying land in Surf Breeze?"

Luke smiled a little. He'd known that his father had heard the news. After all, it's what they had been fighting about when Cassey had broken in.

He took his time and sat down in the chair across from his father. "I told you." He paused, waiting for the irritation to leave his father's face. Instead, it intensified. "I'm using my inheritance to build a hotel."

"The hell you are." His father slammed his hands down on his desk and stood, his face going a deep shade of red. "You've known my plans for over a year. This goes against the family, and I won't stand by and watch you destroy everything I've worked hard for."

"You." He watched his father start pacing in front of the large windows overlooking the clear-skied beaches. "Everything *you've* worked hard for. Great-granddad won this place by chance. Grandpa worked his whole life to make it what it is today, and you've maintained it." He stood. "I don't want to be a maintenance man. I want to set out on my own, using my own skills. If I succeed or fail, it's on me."

"You're doing this because of that girl." His father turned on him.

Luke shook his head. "No." He thought about it. "Well, maybe Cassey had a little to do with it. I'm doing this because I'm tired of being in your shadow. Of being in Calvin's shadow. He was the son who was supposed to be by your side, not me. I want to make something of myself. Find out who Luke Callaway is and maybe make a living out of something I love."

That seemed to throw his father off. He stood across from him, looking at Luke like he was someone he didn't know.

"What about the plans to expand Crystal Shores?"

"You're fighting a losing battle in Surf Breeze.

193

Besides, you're going to need the locals behind you and destroying something that's been around longer than most of them isn't the way to go about it."

His father crossed his arms and turned his back on him to look out the windows. Luke walked up beside him, looking down at the people and families playing on the cold beach. As they stood there in silence, he realized that for the first time in his life, he'd told his father exactly how he felt.

As he drove the lone road to Surf Breeze later that day, he wondered what it would take for his father to trust him completely. He wasn't going to fool himself into believing his father would stop trying to persuade him to follow his plans. He knew it was only a matter of his father recovering before he would try his next scheme.

If he knew his father, by the time he made it back to Cassey, he would already have a new plan in place. Which got him thinking about how he could secure his future, their future.

He'd fallen for her, and hard. There was hardly a moment that went by during the day that he wasn't thinking about her. He knew she was still under the impression that they were just having a physical relationship, but he had plans to show her he meant to stick around.

Deciding to make the first move tonight, he tried to stay within the speed limit, though he wanted to rush back to her and start their future.

Cassey stood back and watched the band set up. Friday night was her favorite night. Many people who lived close by would travel across the big bridge and highway to Surf Breeze and enjoy an evening out. Since her place had some of the best live music in town, a lot of the locals ended up there. She knew most of them by name; they all knew her. Because it was now officially off-season, the crowd in the bar and grill was down to just over two dozen. All in all, not a bad night.

Actually, this last week, since opening her doors again, she'd seen an increase in traffic. Locals came out in droves to support her, stopping by to chat with her and let her know they were behind her. Even some people she hadn't seen since school showed up.

It was nice to see everyone again and to feel the support.

Too many times during the week, she'd wished that Luke was there. Even though she spent almost an hour each evening on the phone with him, she tried to persuade herself that she wasn't becoming attached to him. She knew she needed to sort out her feelings sooner or later but tried to keep herself busy so that she didn't have too much time to think about it.

He was due back later that evening, and she

tried to not watch the front door, but her eyes scanned the crowd, looking for his dark eyes and sexy smile.

After the band started playing, she headed to her office for a break with a Coke in her hand. Tonight was a two-Coke kind of evening, so she had to counteract the sugar with a sandwich from the kitchen. As she sat at her desk, eating her turkey on wheat and sipping her second Coke, she noticed the large envelope that she'd forgotten about.

Ripping it open, she pulled out the contents and completely lost her appetite. She was still sitting there when Luke walked in over an hour later.

"Hey." He smiled and walked across the room to sit on her couch. He rested his head back and closed his eyes. "Am I glad that week is over. You won't believe the lengths my father went to avoid talking to me." He chuckled and then looked up at her. "What?" He sat up, looking at her more closely. "What's wrong?"

"You didn't have to come back down here, you know," she said, trying to hide all the emotions that had flooded her since opening the envelope.

"I know," he said, looking at her cautiously. "I want to be here, with you."

"Yes, but if you were having a good time with your family, you should have stayed."

"Cassey, what's this all about? I told you how my trip went. How I dreaded being there, having to talk to my father."

She shook her head, trying to figure out why all of a sudden she cared so much. "I don't like being lied to."

He leaned back and blinked a few times. "Is this about the land I've bought?"

She continued to look at him. So there was more than one secret he'd been keeping from her.

"Listen..." He leaned forward again. "I was trying to keep it a surprise. At least until everything was finalized. There's still so much that needs to be done, so many chances of it all falling through."

She shook her head, unsure of what he was talking about.

"I'd hoped to surprise you this next week, once I received the final building permit."

"Permit?" Her head was swimming now. She was trying to keep up with him, but all she could focus on were the pictures lying in her lap.

"For the hotel." He frowned. "This isn't about the hotel I'm building in Surf Breeze?"

She stood slowly, and the cluster of pictures of Luke and a very beautiful blonde woman fell to the floor.

"You're building a hotel in Surf Breeze?" When he nodded, she stepped from behind her desk. "And you kept it from me just in case something fell through?" He nodded again. She walked towards the door, her anger showing on her face. Her hands shook as she reached for the door handle.

How had she let him get this close so fast? It was less than three months ago that she'd found him asleep behind her desk. And now she realized she'd totally fallen in love with him, and he was doing exactly what she'd known he would—break her heart.

"I don't know what your motives are, but I'm tired of being lied to. You can show yourself out." She turned and walked out, but instead of heading back downstairs, she walked up the stairs towards her apartment. Her head hurt now and she just wanted to go back to her room and cry herself dry.

By the time she made it to her door, Luke was there, spinning her around.

"What are these?" He held up the pictures she'd been holding a few moments ago.

"They appear to be pictures of you in the last few days." She pushed on his chest and frowned when he didn't budge an inch. "If you were done with all this"—she motioned around her, flinging her arms wildly—"all you had to do was say so. I don't like being lied to or misled. Why don't you explain why someone is sending them to me, while you're at it."

He stepped back, a frown on his lips as a crease appeared between his eyebrows. "I can't believe him." He shook his head. "Well, damn."

She crossed her arms over her chest as he stood there. Then he shocked her by starting to laugh.

"What?" She started to feel her energy disappear. Reaching up, she rubbed her forehead.

"I'm so sorry, babe." He dropped the photos and took her shoulders in his hands. She tried to jerk away, but she was still pinned to her door. "Some of those are from this weekend, but the more…intimate ones are from several years ago. My father thought he could distract me by inviting my ex-girlfriend Angela and her mother down for the week. There's nothing going on between us. Honestly." He pulled her close. "I spent a miserable week trying to get my father alone and fighting off the attentions of Angela and our matchmaking mothers. I wanted to be here, with you." He smiled down at her and she could see the weariness in his eyes.

She'd known it. After all, he'd spent the nights heating her up over the phone. He'd called or texted her a dozen or more times each day. She felt terrible, until she remembered he was building a hotel in Surf Breeze and this was the first she'd heard of it.

"I believe you about the pictures, but that doesn't negate the fact that I'm hurt about your plans to build a hotel. Did your father change his plans?" She waited, keeping her body stiff for what was coming next.

He shook his head and ran his hand down her hair. "Let's go inside and I'll tell you all about it."

When they walked in, she went to the fridge and pulled out two cans of Coke. Popping the top of hers, she took a large sip and closed her eyes. Why was it that when life looked bad, the drink always made her feels more stable?

"Feel better?" Luke asked as he leaned against the countertop, looking at her.

She nodded and held out a can for him. He took it and her hand and pulled her into the living room, where they sat on the couch.

"Since I met you, I've been doing a lot of thinking." He took a drink of his Coke and then set it on the glass coffee table. "I thought that I was stuck doing and being what my father wanted me to be. Working for the family's business, being one of my father's minions, with no real future." He turned and looked at her. "Then I met you." A smile crept onto his face and his eyes grew darker. "You showed me that I could take a chance at what I wanted." He took the can of Coke from her hands and set it on the table. Taking her hands in his, he turned until they were looking into each other's eyes. "I never thought that I would get a chance at happiness. Not after Calvin died. I always imagined I'd be a slave to my father. You gave me the courage to go after what I wanted. And," he chuckled, "it turns out that what I want is to own my very own hotel. Go figure." He shook his head.

"It makes sense." She tried to smile.

"I suppose." He shrugged his shoulders. "I found some land on the edge of town. After driving by it, I went to my grandfather and asked him to release my inheritance. I showed him a business plan that I had written up." He shook his head. "Damn if the old man wasn't proud of me and gave me his full cooperation. Even told me that if Dad gave me any problems, to talk to him. It's the first time in my life that I truly felt like part of the family." He leaned back and looked out her window at the dark courtyard. "My father found out, somehow." He shrugged his shoulders again and looked over at her. "That's the conversation you interrupted. Thank you for that, by the way." He smiled.

"How did he take it now that you've had a chance to talk to him?" she asked.

He shook his head. "Pretty much the same as he did the first time we talked about it. Although, I did get a chance to explain myself a lot further. There was a moment I thought he understood, but..." He shrugged his shoulders. "We'll see how it goes."

She looked down at their joined hands, not sure when she'd started playing with his fingers. "I'm sorry. I know how hurtful parents can be."

He smiled at her and pulled her closer. "I've never felt this way about anyone else."

She tried to pull back, not sure if she wanted to hear what she knew was coming next. She'd been trying to put if off for so long, even knowing she couldn't stop it from coming.

"No," he said lightly. "Don't pull away."

When she hesitated, he took advantage of her hesitation and tugged on her arm until she sat across his lap. She found herself looking into the deep rich pools of his eyes, transfixed by the tenderness she saw there.

"Cassey, I've never felt this way for anyone else. My whole life I've waited and wanted someone like you to come along. I know this started out as just a convenience, but we can't fool ourselves any longer. We've become so much more, and I want our relationship to continue to grow."

"Luke—" Her hands went to his chest, trying to hold him back, trying to hold what she felt back as well.

"No, don't say anything just yet." He pulled her close. "Let me show you how I feel. Let me be with you tonight. I just want to be with you." He leaned his head down and took her lips gently.

In the couple of months that they'd been together, there had been plenty of passion, speed, and desire. But this was the first time she'd felt tenderness and love so strongly. She didn't quite know what to do with the desire that built up. It was different than any other she'd ever felt.

202

No one had ever shown her this much love, ever.

Chapter Fourteen

When she reached for him, he knew she wanted speed. Why had he never realized that she had been avoiding intimacy? Oh, sure, they'd had sex plenty of times, but he realized he hadn't shown her true tenderness and that's what he wanted to give her now.

He knew it was going to kill him, going so slow, but he was willing to suffer if it meant showing her how he felt.

Gathering her up, he carried her towards the bedroom. He smiled as she wrapped her arms around his neck. When she started to object, he took her lips again in a slow kiss that caused him to stop in the hallway. His arms shook with desire, and he tried to keep himself in check and slow himself down.

When they finally made it into the bedroom, he slid her down until she stood in front of him. His hands ran over her subtle curves until she moaned and started tugging at his shirt and jeans.

Taking her hands in his, he backed her up until her knees hit the bed. "I'm going to make love to you all night," he whispered into her ear.

Her head fell back as her eyes closed. Bending down, he placed soft kisses along the column of her neck, running his lips over her heated skin until he felt tiny bumps rise all over her skin.

"Please, Luke." She tossed her head back up and grabbed his hair.

How could he have known that driving her crazy with tenderness would only make him want to show her more? He smiled at her and stepped back, shaking his head.

"My way, remember? Remove your clothes for me." When she started to yank the top over her head, he stopped her. "No, slowly."

She groaned and shut her eyes. "You're killing me." He smiled and when she just looked at him, he could see the desire burning in those clear eyes.

"Do it," he said quietly. She began to move, taking her shirt up inch by inch, exposing the soft skin underneath. He watched in amazement as her breasts came into view. His breath hitched and lodged in his chest.

"You are beautiful beyond words." He took a

step closer, but she shook her head.

"I'm not done." She smiled and, at that moment, he realized he'd lost control of the situation. She slowly started to pull her skirt down her legs in an erotic striptease. Next, she slid her bra straps down her shoulders and then reached around and unhooked it, tossing it on the floor beside him. Her smile grew as she cupped herself, moaning and tilting her head back as she ran her fingers over her skin.

"Tell me how it feels," he said, staring at her, watching her every move. He realized he would have gladly done anything for her at that moment. All she needed to do was ask.

"Soft." She smiled at him. "Warm," she moaned.

He watched as she slowly moved a hand down her ribs and her flat stomach until she reached her silk panties.

"Yes," he moaned, "touch yourself."

She looked into his eyes and nodded to him. "You're turn."

Now it was him who was rushing to remove his clothes.

"No," she broke in, "slowly."

His fingers shook as he flipped open button after button. It was driving him mad watching her fingers run over her skin. When she started to peel off her panties, he stood in front of her with only his socks and boxers on.

"Wait." She held up her hands and nodded to him. "Your turn."

"What?" He blinked a few times.

She ran her hands over her chest. "Now you."

He chuckled. "Somehow I don't think it has the same effect."

"For you, maybe." She smiled.

He shrugged his shoulder and ran his hands over his chest, following her motions. When she reached her sex, he smiled. "This I can do." He dropped his boxers and heard her breath catch.

"Beautiful," she whispered.

He stepped closer to her, reaching out for her. He cupped her face in his hands as he laid his lips gently on hers. "So soft," he said as he ran his hands down her sides. "You smell like flowers and taste like honey," he moaned as he ran his mouth over her skin.

Slowly, he laid her back on the bed until she looked up at him, her gray eyes going darker. "Cassey…" He felt the words clog in his throat. Instead of speaking, he moved above her as her hands reached for him.

"I know." She closed her eyes and he thought he saw a tear roll from the corner of her eye to the mattress below.

After torturing himself by running his hands slowly over her, he slid into her, and said the words he'd been wanting to tell her.

Cassey's head was spinning. She'd slowed her breathing down but still felt too lightheaded to open her eyes. What had Luke done to her?

"You okay?" Even just the richness of his voice sent waves of desire through her body.

Realizing she didn't trust her voice, she nodded and squeezed her eyes shut tighter. When she finally opened them, it was to see Luke smiling down at her.

"What?" she asked, trying to sit up. He held her in place and shook his head.

"You can't avoid it, you know."

"I have no idea what you're talking about." She tried to push him away, but he just laughed and plopped his full weight on her, pinning her to the mattress.

"Ugh! You weigh a ton." She tried to shove him off as he laughed. "Get off."

He was laughing harder now. "Not until you promise me you won't avoid it."

"Stop," she squealed as he buried his nose in

her neck and started nibbling on her. By the time he pulled back and looked at her, she was laughing too hard to say anything.

"Do you promise?" he asked and before she knew what she was doing, she'd nodded in agreement.

"Perfect." He jumped off the bed and pulled her up with him. "I'm starved," he said as he started tugging her towards the kitchen.

"Luke," she squealed, "clothes first!" He just laughed even more.

After making some quick peanut butter and jelly sandwiches, they retreated back to the warmth of the bed and talked. She was avoiding having the conversation and did everything she could to distract Luke from talking about the three words he'd mentioned less than an hour ago.

"You're stalling," he said, setting his plate aside. "You're talking about everything but what needs to be said."

He was right. She couldn't deny her emotions any more. But then she found something that took his mind off the conversation completely.

"Oh," she said, taking the last bite of her sandwich. "I'd almost forgotten. I'm supposed to invite you to Spring Haven for Thanksgiving this Thursday." She smiled when she noticed his eyes go blank. "My Aunt Julie is the best cook in the county."

"Thanksgiving?" He got a funny look on his face and she wondered if she'd made a mistake asking him.

"Yes, you don't have to—"

"I'd love to." His smile grew and he reached for her. Setting her plate aside, he slid them down until they fit tight together.

"You've mentioned your aunt and father, but haven't spoken much of your mother. Mrs. Grayton?"

She sighed and was thankful the conversation had turned. "Elizabeth Grayton was the strongest woman I've ever known." She rested her head back against his shoulder and enjoyed the feeling of his fingers combing her long hair away from her face. "When I first met her, her cancer was in remission. It took several years for it to come back and for her to pass from it." She smiled slightly. "Never once in all that time did I see that woman complain or frown. She didn't shed a tear or get angry at her circumstances."

"I'm sorry," he said, lightly.

She nodded. "That woman taught us more about suffering and patience than any other could. One of the reasons the Graytons took us all in was because of Elizabeth's and Mark's own childhoods. It's the reason all of us devote as much as we can into the home that Roman has built, the reason he has continued on with our family's dream."

"Everyone sounds wonderful. Since I've already met Marcus and Cole, I can't wait to meet everyone else."

She laughed. "You'll regret those words."

Less than a week later, she was sitting around the large maple dining table, surrounded by a bunch of crazy people, and laughing harder than she had in a long time. Her brothers were a constant source of entertainment. She could hardly remember a time that the three of them had been together that they hadn't had her smiling like a loon.

Of course, Luke was right there in the middle of it all. Not only did he look like he fit in, but he sounded and acted a lot like her brothers as they joked with her Aunt Julie and her father about one thing or another.

"You really didn't do that, did you?" he asked, looking over at her. She'd lost track of their conversation minutes before when she'd been transfixed by the way Luke was smiling. He looked like he was really enjoying himself.

"What?" She felt her breathing quicken and quickly took a sip of her wine to cover the anxiety.

He leaned closer to her, his smile getting bigger. "Run from here to the middle of town, wearing nothing but a hula skirt and coconuts."

She glared at her brothers then closed her eyes, remembering. "Yes, but it wasn't my fault," she said as everyone burst into laughter. "They locked me out of the house and bet me that they would do all my chores and be my own personal slaves for a whole month if I did it." She tried not to laugh. She'd been thirteen and had just enough pride to not want to lose a bet. She smiled, remembering seeing her brothers do her every bidding. They'd been great sports about it, and since they and Marissa had followed her the entire way, they had a wonderful picture of the five of them standing in front of town hall, her brothers' arms around her shoulders as she wore the hula skirt and coconuts from her school play.

The rest of the evening went very well. She tried not to stare at Luke and kept her heart hidden from her family, as usual.

As they were sitting around the fire in the living room, watching a football game, Luke's cell phone rang. She watched him flip it out and frown down at it, and then he stood and excused himself.

She tried not to watch him pace on the front porch as he talked, most likely to someone from his family. When he came in, she could see the spark had left his eyes.

It took a few minutes before they were finally alone, and she immediately asked if everything was all right.

"Yes. I knew they'd be upset that I was

spending the holiday with your family, but I didn't know how much." He took her hand and they stepped outside onto the front porch. The night breeze was cool as the wind whipped through her hair. He pulled off his jacket and put it over the light sweater she was wearing. Then he walked to the railing and leaned on it. "I like it here. I can just imagine you and your brothers growing up here. Chasing each other in the yard, running through the house." He turned and smiled at her. "Makes me a little envious."

She walked over to him and placed a hand on his knee. Looking up into his eyes. "I'm sorry they were upset."

He shrugged his shoulders and turned to look off into the dark night.

Even though fall along the Gulf Coast wasn't very cold, they still had chilly nights. Even the bugs had decreased during the small cold front they were having now. The grass was still green, and most of the trees still had leaves, but the chill in the wind guaranteed they were in for some rain later that night.

"It's not like we spend holidays together. It's been years since we've had a Thanksgiving meal together. Even then, it was nothing like that." He nodded to the large windows, where they could see her brothers yelling at the football game. They were cheering and most likely taking bets as to which team would score next.

214

"I'm sorry," she said, pulling his face towards hers. "I know how it feels. I wish it was different for you."

He smiled and ran his fingers through her hair. "I'm so lucky to have you. To be here with you." He leaned down and placed a soft kiss on her lips. "I know you don't want to hear it, but I love you. I love being here with your family, with you."

She smiled. "I think I'm getting used to hearing it." It was true. Since that night almost a week ago when he'd first uttered those words, he'd made a point to say them to her as often as he could. She still didn't know if there would be a day when she would easily be able to say it back to him. After all, she'd never said it to any man before.

"I'd like your permission to move in to your place. You know, full-time."

She thought about it for a moment. He was already practically living at her place. His clothes hung in the spare bedroom closet, and several items were in her medicine cabinet.

Just then, there was a loud shout from inside the house. They both looked over to see Marcus jumping up and down. Cole still had his arm in a sling, but he was pumping his other fist in the air and the two of them fist-bumped over Roman's head.

"Looks like Roman lost the bet," she said, smiling at the scene her family made. Her aunt and father were shaking their heads as they laughed at the three of them. "It's rare that he loses," she said, turning back towards Luke.

"I like them a lot," he said.

"That's nice. I can tell they like you, too."

"Shall we head back in? I'm dying to know the score." She smiled.

Chapter Fifteen

The weeks between Thanksgiving and Christmas were busy for him. Luke found it hard to find time to get back down to Emerald Beach. He wanted to finish the talk with his father and maybe see what he was up to. It wasn't like his father to sit back and not have a plan in motion.

As he drove the highway, he thought of his own plans, plans that included asking Cassey to marry him. He thought the Christmas holiday was the best time. He could just imagine asking her on the beach.

She had yet to say she loved him back, and every time he told her, a strange look would cross her face. He considered himself to be a very patient man, but he really wished she would tell him what was going on, why she held herself back like that. He could tell that he mattered to her; after all, she'd let him officially move in, something that had never happened before, according to Wendy. And according to her brothers, something they thought would never happen.

When he drove up to the hotel, he noticed his father's car wasn't parked out front. Frowning, he walked into the building and was quickly approached by one of the employees.

"Oh, Mr. Wallace, I'm so sorry to hear about your father." She looked over her shoulder, then back at him. "Will you tell him that all of us here are pulling for him to get better?"

"What are you talking about?" He had a sinking feeling in his gut and after gazing around the lobby, he realized everyone was looking at him funny.

Less than an hour later he stood over his father, a deep frown on his lips as he looked at the man who had never been sick a day in his life. A stroke at the age of fifty-eight. Luke hadn't seen it coming. Nor had anyone else, including his mother, who stood next to him, holding his hand.

"We were having tea with the DeFords. You remember, the nice couple who owned the condo next to ours in Maui. Anyway, your father had been feeling just a little under the weather since Thanksgiving." His mother looked down at his father as he slept in a drugged state. She shook her head as a tear fell down her cheek. "He just slumped over. At first I thought he was joking," She reached up and wiped the tear away quickly.

"What have the doctors said?"

"That he's stable now." She shook her head. "They say he might have some permanent damage, but they'll know more once he wakes up."

"He hasn't woken yet?"

"No." She quickly dashed away some more tears.

"Mom—" He started to apologize for not being there, but just then his phone beeped. Seeing Cassey's number, he excused himself from the room.

"Hey, so I was wondering if you were going to stay up there tonight?"

"Yes, Cassey, my father's had a stroke," he blurted out. He didn't know what he felt; his emotions were hard to explain. He was feeling anger and sadness at the same time. If his father hadn't been such a workaholic his whole life, maybe he wouldn't have had the stroke.

"Oh, no. Luke, I'm so sorry. What hospital?"

He told her. "I'll be there soon. I'm so sorry. Do you need anything?" she asked.

"No, just you." He couldn't explain it, but he just knew that with her by his side, he could handle everything he had to.

"I'll be there. Give me an hour to tie up some loose ends around here first."

When he walked back into the room, his father's eyes were open. His mother was sitting by his side, tears coming down her face.

It was so hard to explain, but he wished he could be anywhere but in that room at that moment.

"See, here he is Jeffery. I told you he had come." His mother patted his father's hand. "I just called for a nurse," she said when he made a move towards the door to do so.

He stood aside as several nurses came in, followed by a doctor a few minutes later. He watched as everyone bustled around his father. Every time someone moved aside, he noticed that his father's eyes were glued to him. Then they were being asked to step outside while they examined his father more closely.

Standing in the hall, hugging his mother, he realized he still hadn't said anything to her. She just hung on his shirt and cried silently.

It took almost fifteen minutes before the doctor walked out of the room again.

"Well?" His mother gripped his arm tightly. "How is Jeffery?"

"Your husband has suffered a mild stroke." His mother sniffled. "He's young and fit, which he has in his favor. But he has suffered some damage.

Whether it's temporary or permanent, I can't say; it's still too early to tell. He'll need to stay here until we see improvements. Once he goes home, he'll have to be looked after until he's back on his feet."

"What about work?" Luke blurted out.

The doctor shook his head. "I'm not sure. He has a long road to recovery ahead of him."

His mother gripped his arm even tighter. "Can we go back in?"

"Yes, but only family at this time. We'll move him to a more private room in the morning."

When they walked in the room again, his mother dropped his arm and rushed to his father's side.

"I'm here, Jeffery," she said, over and over. "Luke is here, too," she said, when she noticed his eyes on his son. "Come over here, Luke. Say something to your father."

Luke moved closer to the bed. His father lay there, looking old and frail for the first time in his memory.

"I'm here," he said, hearing his voice crack a little.

"Calvin?" his father's eyes lit up and Luke's heart broke a little more.

221

Cassey hurried to the elevator and was surprised to see Luke standing in front of the doors, two cups of coffee in his hands.

"Luke," she called out as the doors opened. Rushing, she made it inside just before the doors closed.

"Hey." He smiled down at her after blinking a few times.

"Are you okay?" she asked, helping him with the coffee.

"Yeah. I'm glad you're here."

"How's your father?"

"He's awake." He looked over as the elevator started beeping, then leaned over and pushed the button for the fifth floor. "It was a mild stroke. Looks like he'll have to stay here for a few days."

"Luke, I'm so sorry." She took his free hand in hers and watched him nod in response.

"You didn't have to come down here."

He looked so sad that she wrapped her free arm around his waist. "I wanted to be here with you."

When they walked into his father's room, she saw his mother for the first time. She didn't know why she hadn't thought that the woman would be there, but the thought just hadn't crossed her mind. She was beautiful. Her dark hair was shoulder length and styled in a fashionable bob. She wore silk white pants with a matching top and a teal scarf wrapped around her neck. Large diamond earrings dangled from her ears and the huge rings on her fingers were probably worth enough money to feed a small country.

"Cassey, this is my mother, Sophia Callaway. Mother, this is Cassey Grayton, my girlfriend." He handed his mother the coffee.

Cassey noticed that Mrs. Callaway's hand paused as she reached for the cup Luke offered.

"Oh," the woman said, looking down at her husband, who appeared to be sleeping. "Nice to meet you," she said in a more stressed voice. "I'm sorry; they won't allow you to stay in this room."

"It's okay. I was just helping Luke with the coffee," Cassey said, handing Luke his cup, then turning to go. She knew when she wasn't welcome.

"Cass." Luke took her hand. "Stay. Mother, don't be rude. Cassey drove all the way down here to be with me. To see how father was."

Mrs. Callaway looked between her and her husband. "Well, I'm sure it won't hurt if you stay for a few minutes."

"Would you like something to drink?" Luke held out his cup.

"No, thank you. I just wanted to make sure everything was okay." She felt awkward and wished Luke had let her leave. Maybe she'd go sit outside or take a walk on the beach until he left for the night.

"Why don't you two go ahead and call it a night," his mother said all of a sudden. "I'll sit here with Jeffery until they kick me out."

"Are you sure?" Luke looked a little relieved.

"Yes." She set her coffee down, sat next to her husband, and picked up his hand. "Go, I'll be fine."

When they walked out of the hospital, it was raining pretty hard. It had sprinkled all the way from Surf Breeze, but this was a downpour. They stood in the doorway of the hospital, waiting for it to lighten up.

"Why don't we leave my car here overnight and take yours to the hotel?" he suggested. He pulled his coat up over his collar. "Let's make a run for it. I don't think it's going to let up soon."

They dashed for her car, holding hands. She unlocked it a few feet away and jumped in behind the wheel. Luke jumped in next to her and shook the rain from his hair.

She reached over to start the car, but he stopped her and pulled her across the console towards him. The hug was desperate and moved something deep inside her.

"Sorry," he said a few minutes later when he pulled away. "But I needed that."

She smiled at him. "Are you okay?"

He nodded. "Yeah. I could use some food though."

"Okay, where to?" She started the car and waited.

"The hotel. I keep a room there. We can order room service."

"Okay." She drove out of the parking lot. The rain had yet to lighten up and now it was even lightning as well. She drove slowly across town towards the large hotel. When they pulled into the parking garage, he pointed her towards his private parking spot.

They walked towards the elevators in silence. She didn't know what to say to him. It was good news that his father would recover, but hearing that it would be a long road to recovery had caused many questions to pop into her head. Did that mean he would be staying to run the hotel? Did this change their relationship?

They rode the elevator to the top floor and when she walked out, she was shocked to see only two doors on this level.

"The other unit belongs to my parents." He nodded towards the double doors at the end of the hallway.

225

"You said you kept a room," she said a few minutes later, looking around the large apartment. "I didn't know you had an apartment here."

He shrugged. "When you've lived in the same place your whole life, you tend to not think of it as anything but home." He walked over to the glass refrigerators and pulled out a bottle of beer. "Would you like something? There's wine, beer." He bent down and opened the bottom drawer. "Coke?" He took one out for her.

"Yes, thanks." She popped it open and took a sip. He'd yet to take a drink of his beer, but instead was just watching her.

"I'm really glad you came. I needed you so much. I just need you," he said, just before he took the can from her and set his beer and the Coke down on the bar. Then he was kissing her with so much feeling, she had no choice but to hold onto him and let him take what he needed from her.

Later, as they lay in his large bed, he talked to her and told her what had happened at the hospital, how his father had mistaken him for his brother.

"I'm sure it was just the drugs talking."

"Yeah, I know you're right, but it doesn't take away the fact that his eyes lit up." He shook his head as he continued to run his fingers through her hair. "It still hurt."

"He doesn't know what a great son he still has." She sat up a little. "Neither of them does. I can see it in their eyes." She looked down at him, lying on

226

the bed with the sheets covering his hips. His arm rested behind his head as he looked at her. She shook her head. "I didn't get a chance to meet Calvin, and I'm sure he was a great man." She sat up a little more and made sure to look into his eyes. "But they have one of the best sons staring them right in the face and they can't see beyond their noses."

His smile was slow to form, but when it did, it was the sweetest thing she'd seen all day.

"What do you say to some room delivery?"

She smiled back. "Can this place make a decent pizza and banana splits?"

He laughed. "Some of the best on the gulf."

Chapter Sixteen

Cassey woke up enveloped by Luke and the thick warm blankets. His warm smell surrounded her, filling the whole room. When she thought about him not being there when she woke, her gut would twist and ache. Was he going to be staying on? There were so many questions left unanswered from last night. She knew early morning wasn't the best time to ask everything she wanted to, but she doubted she could wait much longer.

"What has you so tense this morning?" he murmured into her ear.

She sighed and then smiled. It was nice that he knew her so well. In the past, she'd never reached this level in her relationships. She found that she liked knowing his moods as well.

It had been hard to gauge his moods at first, but after a few weeks, she had picked up on the subtle changes in his eyes and face when his moods changed.

She rolled over until she could look him directly in the eyes. "Will you be staying here until your father recovers?"

His dark eyes looked back at her, and she couldn't tell what he was thinking.

"I suppose I will have to stay on, at least until he goes home." He frowned a little.

"Don't you need to run the business until he can go back?"

"No, my father has a whole floor of competent employees who can handle it until he gets back on his feet." He brushed a strand of her hair away from her eyes. "I plan on going back to Surf Breeze as soon as possible. I have my own business to tend to now. We break ground in less than a week. We'd better head out. I'm sure they've moved him to another room by now."

They grabbed a quick breakfast downstairs, where he was approached by over a dozen employees who all wished his father a speedy recovery.

It was close to nine when they walked into his father's private room. His mother was sitting in the chair in the corner, a book in her lap.

"Oh, there you are. I was beginning to wonder

if you were going to make it."

"How's he doing?" Luke asked.

"He's stable. The doctors have come and gone several times. All of them say the same thing." She set the book down and hugged Luke.

"Have you had breakfast?" he asked.

"Yes, don't you worry about me. Now, Calley, sit down and tell me all about yourself."

"It's Cassey, Mother," Luke corrected.

"Yes, of course. Sorry, dear." His mother motioned to another chair near hers. "Sit, please."

Cassey walked over and sat next to the woman, feeling completely out of place. Luke's mother was wearing a pale green skirt and blazer, the pearls wrapped around her neck were undoubtedly real, and she didn't have a hair out of place.

She looked down at her jeans and sweatshirt and wished she'd dressed a little better. She also wished that she'd thought to bring an umbrella, since it had still been raining this morning. Her hair was frizzed, and her makeup was probably running from the downpour they'd sprinted through to get into the hospital.

"Now, what is it you do, dear?"

"Cassey owns Boardwalk Bar and Grill in Surf Breeze. You know, the one dad's been trying to buy for the last year," Luke broke in as he shuffled a chair closer to hers.

"Oh, that's nice." Cassey could see the interest leave her face.

"I hope Mr. Callaway will make a speedy recovery."

"Oh, I'm sure he will. He was fit as a fiddle before." She frowned and looked at her sleeping husband. "Well now, tell me about your parents. I believe I knew your father a long time ago."

"Mark Grayton?"

She nodded her head. "I grew up in Spring Haven; we were in the same class in school."

Cassey smiled. Here she'd thought that the woman had grown up with a silver spoon in her mouth. Looking at her, Cassey had a hard time imagining the woman sitting in the broken down stands at the high school football field, rooting for the Fighting Bulldogs.

Mrs. Callaway laughed. "Oh, the times we had sneaking out to Orsborn Orchards. They had this pond, with a dock floating in the middle. One Fourth of July, we snuck over a hundred kids out there in his pond. Someone had heard that old Mr. Orsborn was going to be gone for the weekend." She smiled, leaned closer, and tapped Cassey's knee. "We may not have had cell phones back then, but word spread like wildfire. Well, of course, the information was false. When Mr. Orsborn showed up, everyone started to scatter, until he pulled off his shirt and jumped in to the water with everyone else. Well, he sat there and ate and drank and enjoyed the day like he'd thrown the party himself."

Cassey laughed. "Mr. Orsborn now hosts the biggest Fourth of July party in town. I'd wondered where that tradition started."

By the time they headed back to the hotel later that evening, Cassey was sure she'd just made a new friend. Luke's dad woke several times during the day. Each time Cassey would step outside since she didn't want to cause him any stress.

"I think my mother likes you more than she likes me," Luke said as they walked into his apartment.

"I like her, too. I had no idea your mother was a Bulldog."

"Pardon me?" He turned and gave her a funny look and she laughed.

"A Spring Haven Bulldog. Our school mascot."

"Oh," he chuckled. "Do you know that she talked to you today more than she has ever talked to me?"

Cassey shook her head and frowned. "I'm sorry."

He smiled. "Don't be. It's nice knowing that even if my father won't give you a chance, at least my mother has."

He walked over to her and wrapped his arms around her waist. "I like knowing that at least one

233

of my parents approves of us."

She smiled and stood up on her toes. "I know you've won over my entire family. Dad's asking if you'll be back for Christmas."

Luke frowned. "I think I might have to pass."

"I understand." She tried hard not to let the sadness show in her eyes.

"Maybe you can come down here for a few days?"

She nodded. She was finding it too difficult to talk. "I hate to leave, but I've a million things to do before I take off next week."

He nodded then looked down at her mouth. "I wish you could stay."

She nodded just before he kissed her slowly, showing her how much he wished it.

On her drive home, she tried not to let the fact that she'd become entirely too attached to him dominate her mind.

She arrived back at her place, and chaos consumed the rest of the next few days. Two of the heater units stopped working, leaving the place a little too chilly for her or her customers' liking. She had to hire a local company to replace the units, which ate into her savings a little more.

Then just three days before Christmas, she was on damage control back in the kitchen. Her head chef, Sam, had caught his wife having an affair and wasn't in the mood to either cook or be civilized to any of the other staff. Cassey had no alternative but to send him home and help in the kitchen herself.

She still hadn't had any time to get the rest of her Christmas shopping done, and more important, she still hadn't had time to get Luke anything yet.

They'd talked to each other every day. His father had been moved home and, with the help of two full-time nurses, he was on the mend.

According to Luke, he still called him Calvin and thus far that was the only word he'd said since waking.

She was in the kitchen, cleaning up after the evening shift, getting ready to close the place down for Christmas, when her cell rang.

Smiling, she answered it. "Hi, I was just thinking about you."

Luke chuckled. "Good things, I hope."

"Always. How's your dad?"

He sighed and she could tell things were the same. "Pretty much the same. I really wanted to see you for Christmas, but it doesn't look like I'll get out of here until after New Year's."

She tried not to let the disappointment reflect in her voice.

"I can always—"

"No," he interrupted. "Go be with your family."

She couldn't believe that she'd allowed him to be so deeply embedded into her life that just a few days away from him made her feel like a lonely old maid. She found herself tossing and turning because she missed his warmth in the bed. She missed seeing him sit across the table from her during breakfast. She missed his friendship, his laughter, and his touch.

"I miss you," she blurted out, then immediately felt like a stupid high school girl with a crush, something she never remembered feeling before.

"I miss you, too." She could hear the smile in his voice. "Soooo, what are you wearing?"

She laughed.

When Luke hung up the phone with Cassey, he sighed and closed his eyes for just a moment. His family and this job were going to kill him. What he wanted and needed was to be in Surf Breeze with Cassey, working on his own projects and helping Cassey with hers.

"Luke?" His mother peeked into the office. "Oh, there you are. Your father was wondering how things were going."

"Fine, I'll be there shortly to give him an update." Even though his father had only said the word "Calvin" since waking, that didn't mean he hadn't demanded hourly updates. He still had full motion with his fingers and hands and typed faster than most secretaries. Luke was finding it hard to keep up. On several occasions, he'd thought about just leaving. Especially when his father would punch the keys and glare at him like he was stupid.

Since Luke was in control of the business, he'd made a few changes he'd been thinking about since his father had brought him on board almost a year ago. For the most part, his father had a handful of competent employees that could run the place smoothly, so he looked at it all as a great opportunity.

So far, he was seeing great success with his changes. The employees seemed to enjoy the flex shifts he'd implemented, and the office staff really enjoyed being able to work remotely. So far, their productivity was up by almost ten percent.

He'd yet to tell his father any of that, of course, since he didn't want to cause him more stress.

They'd moved their father back into their apartment across from his and had a large hospital bed setup with several machines. Two full-time nurses came and went as well as a staff of physical therapists.

His father still had not regained his speech. He was learning to walk again, slowly, but his left leg dragged a little, causing him to stumble sometimes. He had to use a walker, which Luke could only guess pissed his father off no end.

His mother was treating the whole ordeal like it was some sort of family vacation. She kept a chipper tone and smiled entirely too much.

For his part, he was absolutely miserable. He missed the slower life of Surf Breeze. He missed his hotel project, which was moving forward without him. And mostly, he missed Cassey.

Talking with her each day wasn't helping much. He wanted to hold her, to smell her sweetness, and to see her smile one of those rare smiles she had. He didn't know how much longer he could hold out.

When he talked to his mother about it, she would just pat his arm and ask him to stay just a while longer. He thought she was just enjoying having him around. It was true she knew nothing about running the hotel or staff, but he was sure the place would get along just fine without him. He would leave if it weren't for the guilty look she gave him every time they talked about his father.

His mother was staying busy putting up Christmas decorations everywhere. She'd even had a tree delivered to his place. For his part, he worked in his father's office from morning to nightfall and then dragged himself back to his apartment, desperately wishing to be anywhere but there.

He'd stopped by and picked up his gift for Cassey and couldn't wait until he could watch her open the small box.

Since his father's stroke, he had known what he wanted more than anything in the world. So much had changed in the last few months since he had met Cassey. He no longer felt like he was alone in the world. She's opened a whole new doorway for him to go through. No one had ever done so much for him in his life, except maybe Calvin.

Just then, his phone rang and his thoughts of Cassey and his brother were interrupted by more work. This time it was on his own project.

"Hello?"

"Hey, Luke. It's Marcus. I'm just giving you a heads-up that the inspector will be here Monday. The cement work was completed today and we've got everything covered for the weather we're supposed to have over the holiday weekend."

"Great. Sorry I can't be there myself."

"Don't worry about it. Oh, I'm opening an office above The Lunch Box. Rented the space out so I can hold meetings and all that. Might even get a secretary or two." He chuckled.

"That's good to hear. Shall I meet you there and we can go over the plans in..." He looked at his calendar. "Say late next week?"

"Sure. How's the old man doing?"

"The same." He frowned.

"Well, send him my best."

"Hey, Marcus?"

"Yeah?"

"I wish I could be there with your family this weekend."

"Next time." Marcus chuckled. "That is if you can convince my sister to keep your ugly mug around."

"Oh, I plan on doing just that." He smiled and looked down at the small box as a new plan formed in his head. "You know what? I might just make it up there for Christmas after all."

Chapter Seventeen

When Luke walked into his father's office the next day, he was shocked to see his old man behind the desk. His mother was sitting in the corner quietly reading a book.

"Mom." He nodded to her and continued to walk across the floor towards his father. "Dad, what are you doing here? You're supposed to be on bed rest for the next few weeks."

His father's eyes narrowed. He typed something on his computer and then spun the screen around so he could read it.

"What have you done to my company? Why are half my employees working from home? Where are my weekly reports? What is this about discount meals for employees?"

He sighed and sat down across from his father and started to explain all the changes he'd implemented during his father's absence.

When he walked into his apartment just over ten hours later, he was exhausted. Looking around the large space, he realized he had nothing here he wanted to move with him. All the furnishings, all the decorations had been picked out by the hotel interior decorator years before.

Walking into his bedroom, he thought that the only things he'd take with him were his clothing and a small box of items that had belonged to him and Calvin when they were kids.

He had been so busy all day, explaining everything to his father, that he hadn't told them about getting married. It wasn't as if it had slipped his mind. On the contrary, he couldn't stop thinking about it—being with Cassey, starting a new life with her. It's all he had thought about all day long while his father was reaming him for the changes.

Even after he had explained how productivity was up and employee costs were down, his father had undone everything he'd changed in the last few weeks. It was the biggest slap to the face his father could have given him. Even with all his hard work the last few weeks, his father still wouldn't trust him to handle the business. Which only assured him that his move to Surf Breeze was the best thing he could have ever done.

He picked up the phone to dial Cassey, looking at his watch. It was a quarter to midnight and he knew that on a normal night she would be in the thick of things with still almost an hour until closing time. But since she was spending the holidays with her family, she may have gone to bed earlier. He hoped she would still be awake.

"Hello," she answered in a soft whisper.

"Hi, I miss you." He smiled as he removed his shoes and leaned back on his bed.

"Me, too. How did today go?"

He groaned.

"That good, huh?"

He chuckled. "You've no idea. I just don't get how I came from someone like him. Can you believe that in one day he undid everything I worked hard to accomplish in the last few weeks?"

"Even the flex hours?"

"Yeah. Said that it was a nine-to-five life as far as office personnel."

"Did you mention that some of your connections are overseas?"

"Yup." He shook his head. "I guess my dad is just too old school to realize how big globalization really is."

"Well, just think, by this time next year you will be running your own business how you want.

Some of his employees might even jump ship and join the winning team."

He smiled as he thought about it. "What did you do today?"

She sighed.

"Don't tell me you worked. You took a handful of days off and you spent them glued to the computer, didn't you?"

She laughed. "No, actually, I spent a few hours kicking my brothers' butts in basketball."

"I didn't know you played."

She chuckled, and he realized how much he missed hearing her laugh and seeing the smile on her lips. "I don't. We were playing on the Xbox"

"Oh." He smiled. "I'm pretty good at those games. How about you see if you can kick my butt next time I'm up there."

"It's on."

They talked until the sun started to rise, and then he showered and got ready for another day of dealing with his dad and his high demands.

Cassey was miserable. Here it was the biggest and best holiday of the year and all she could do was sit in the living room at the big house and sigh. Her brothers were acting up and had been kicked out of the house by her aunt, who refused to let them toss the football around. She'd declined to go with them since she didn't feel like losing and putting up with their cheating at the moment.

There was almost an hour before dinner was going to be served, and she just couldn't stand to be cooped up any longer. Grabbing her jacket, she walked out onto the front deck and watched for a while as her brothers tackled one another and tossed the ball around. When they asked her to join again, she told them she was walking to the water's edge. Their pond wasn't as big as Mr. Orsborn's, but it served its purpose and was an excellent swimming hole, nonetheless.

As she walked through the tall grass towards the water, she thought about everything that had changed in the last year.

Her business was still struggling, but she knew that with Luke's plans for his hotel, and the plans they'd made together for her place, things were going to start picking up again after the holidays. It was just a matter of time.

She'd gone almost a whole week without Luke being around and still couldn't figure out why it meant so much to her. She found herself getting more and more depressed.

Her place felt empty, which it had never felt before. Maybe she needed a cat or a small dog to fill the space instead.

She made it to the pond's edge and sat on the large log that her brothers had rolled there one summer to use as a seat. This was one of her happy places. So many fun times had been spent here with her brothers and sister. If she closed her eyes, she could see them all in different stages of their lives. Young, early teen, adulthood. All of them except Marissa. Her sister's image was frozen on the last day she'd ever seen her.

When she heard a snap of a branch behind her, she turned, thinking she'd see one of her brothers. Instead, Luke walked down the path towards her, his hands in the pockets of his worn-out jeans. His brown leather jacket was zipped up. His hair was messy from the wind and he looked troubled.

Immediately, she stood. "What? What's wrong? Is your father—?"

"No." He shook his head. "Dad's resting fine at home with my mother." He stopped beside her and she noticed he didn't reach out to touch her or lean down to kiss her hello. She felt like she'd been slapped in the face.

Instantly, her mind clouded with reasons. Then it dawned on her. He looked troubled because he was coming here to break it off with her. Her shoulders slumped and she felt like her heart stopped for several moments.

"Are you hearing me?" He placed his hands on her shoulders and shook her a little.

"Hmm?" She blinked a few times, clearing the

heartbreak she'd created in her mind and head.

"Where did you just go?" he asked, dropping his hands from her shoulders. Instantly, she felt the loss of the warmth of his touch and wondered if she could continue living without it.

She shook her head and felt her eyes start to sting.

"What are you doing here? I thought you couldn't get away until after New Year's?"

He shrugged his shoulders. "I had to leave. I had to come see you." He turned and walked towards the pond and then stopped after kicking a pebble into the calm water. "If I told you something, would you promise not to freak out?" He turned towards her again.

She felt frozen in her steps. She knew what was coming. Although she'd never had someone break it off with her—she'd always been the one to run away from relationships—she'd always known this day was coming. The day her heart would break beyond repair.

She couldn't speak, so she just nodded, instead.

He took two steps towards her and reached for her. She felt like jolting away, but stood her ground instead.

"I love you. I love you with every ounce of my being. Cassey, I want to be with you for the rest of my life. I want to wake up next to you, see your silvery eyes as they go foggy when I touch you."

247

He ran a finger lightly down her cheek, over her lips slowly, and then down her neck and smiled. "Yes, just like that. I want to know that you feel that way about me, too. I think you do, but I need to know it. Do you feel the same way?" He pulled her close and she could feel his heart beating through their jackets. Maybe it was her own she felt; it was racing like a jackrabbit being chased by a fox.

Her eyes were trapped in his dark brown ones. When he blinked, she was released from the gaze and her eyes wandered over his face. There were dark circles under his eyes, telling her that he hadn't been sleeping well. He looked like he could use a haircut and a shave, which only gave him a dangerous, sexy look.

She knew the answer to his question. She'd known it for weeks, but had been trying to avoid thinking about it. Avoid owning up to it even in her own mind.

She blinked a few times and realized he was silently watching her, waiting for her reply.

"I…" She cleared her throat and saw fear jump into his eyes. Shaking her head, she tried to smile at him. "Be patient, this is the first time I've ever told someone this." His smile was fast and deadly. All the fear and doubt left her, making her feel giddy. "Yes, I love you. I love you more than I want to. I don't think I could ever stop loving you." She laughed when he pulled her close and started spinning in circles.

When he was done, he set her down and his smile fell away. "Now, here comes the hard part."

A burst of laughter escaped her. "That wasn't the hard part?"

He smiled and shook his head, then dropped down on one knee right there by the clear waters of her pond. "Cassey Grayton, my family is selfish and my father runs a business that will do anything it takes to make sure your business goes under so he can take over the boardwalk. I might be tied up for the next few months helping my father run that business. Not to mention trying to get my own business off the ground. I don't know if I'll succeed—"

"Luke," she interrupted, since he was starting to ramble.

"Sorry." He shook his head. "Cassey, will you marry me?"

She smiled. "I think that's a great next step."

He laughed. "Oh, damn." He shook his head. "I forgot. Now I'll have to start all over." He dropped to his knee again. This time as he did so, he pulled out a small black silk box.

Her heart skipped. For some reason, she hadn't thought he'd actually thought about this before today.

"Cassey, will you marry me?" he asked as he opened the lid of the box. The ring was breathtaking. She'd never seen its likeness. Not only was the diamond bigger than any she'd seen, but the titanium band was twisted in a unique way. She couldn't talk this time and just nodded as he stood to place the ring on her finger.

"It's beautiful," she whispered, looking down at the ring.

"I'd like to say it was my grandmother's, but my mother is still wearing that one. Besides, I doubt my father would give it up under the circumstances." He frowned a little.

"It doesn't matter. It's the most beautiful ring I've ever seen." She smiled as she wrapped her arms around his neck and placed a kiss on his lips, which he took deeper.

When they walked into the house just over half an hour later, they were both breathless from the walk and the heated passion they'd shared by the cold waters.

"Guess he found you." Marcus smiled as he shook Luke's hand.

"Yes." She waited until her father walked into the room. "And we're engaged." She held up her finger, showing off the ring.

Everyone looked surprised except Marcus and her father. Her aunt squealed and rushed across the room to hug her. Cole and Roman shook Luke's hand and hugged her.

When her father finally made it over, she thought she saw tears in his eyes. "I can't believe my little girl is getting married. He's a fine man," he said and pulled her aside as Luke talked to her brothers. "You know, he stopped by a few weeks back to ask for your hand. I was so proud. We sat for almost two hours and talked until I finally said yes." He shook his head. "Damn if that man doesn't love you." He smiled.

"Oh, Dad." She hadn't felt the tears in her eyes until he reached up and wiped one away.

"I'm so proud of you," he said and hugged her.

Later that night, as they lay in the small bed of her youth, they talked about the future. He couldn't wait to really be living with her since he'd been away so much since he'd moved in. But, he had to made sure his father was back up to par or at least make sure his employees were running everything smoothly.

"I wish I didn't have to head back tomorrow," Luke said, running his fingers lightly over her shoulders.

"Me, too." She sighed and fell asleep in his arms, dreaming of what life was going to be like in the upcoming weeks.

Chapter Eighteen

When Luke walked into his father's office the next day at a quarter past ten, he noticed two things right away: one, his mother wasn't present and two, his father sat behind his desk in shorts and a T-shirt, which wasn't the norm at all. His father was looking out the large windows as if daydreaming, something he'd never seen him do before now.

"Morning, Dad." He walked over and sat in one of the large chairs. "Where's Mom this morning?"

His father glanced over and looked at him. "She's down at the pool." He nodded his head out the window. "I am going to head down to join her in a while."

The surprise must have registered on his face

because his father smiled slightly and nodded.

"I can see it in your eyes, son," he said and turned back to his computer for just a moment. "There are just a few things I have to get off my chest before I take off. Let's talk about this ring you purchased a little over a month ago." His father turned away from his computer and glanced at him. "Is it for that girl?"

"Yes. I've asked Cassey to marry me and she's said yes." He smiled and crossed his arms over his chest, knowing what was coming next. But his father just looked at him and nodded slowly.

"Fine." He started to turn back towards the windows.

"Fine? What does that even mean, fine?" He leaned forward.

"It means just that. Fine. Luke, I'm not going to interfere with your personal life."

"Really?" he said, standing slowly. "Since when?"

His father smiled slightly. "Since now. Do you know where I spent my morning?"

Luke shook his head.

"Physical therapy. I sat there thinking that this was all just some sort of nasty trick my body was playing on me, a one-time thing that I could easily bounce back from. Then Raul, my physical therapist, laughed at me." His father chuckled. "He's a two-hundred-pound man full of muscles and tattoos, and when he told me that the only way I was going to live to see next year was to change my attitude, it got me thinking. Not only am I not helping my health by trying to control everything, but I've threatened my marriage and my relationship with my only living son." He shook his head and Luke saw his father's shoulders sink a little. Then he stood and walked around his desk. Luke noticed how his father moved slowly.

"Luke, I know that I've not always been the best father, but I want to change that. My physical therapist says that nine out of ten men who continue to live like they did before their first stroke will go on to have another one. And most don't survive their second stroke. Do you know what your mother told me then?"

Luke shook his head and sat back down. He could hardly believe what his father was saying. It was like an alien had taken over his body and was talking to him as a father would.

"She told me that if I didn't change the way I was living, she was going to leave me, because she couldn't live through seeing me like that again." His father's eyes were damp. "That woman has been by my side through a lot of things, and I'll be damned if I'll be the cause of her leaving me now."

Luke smiled as his father shook his head and cleared his throat.

"So, your mother tells me she likes this girl,"

"Cassey."

His father nodded his head. "Cassey. And I'm going to try to give her another chance. Why don't you bring her over for dinner sometime?"

Luke nodded again. It was as if he'd lost all his powers of speech.

"Good. Now if that's settled, can we talk about these changes you've made in my absence?" His father walked back behind his desk as Luke sighed. He didn't want to talk about the changes anymore, not since his father had undone them all.

"I've been looking over some of your changes and well...I think you might have something there."

Luke sat in his father's office for the next few hours and wondered if his father had been body-snatched. Not only had his father reimplemented all the changes he had made over the weeks, but he listened to a few others he'd been proposing over the years.

By the end of the day, his head was spinning. They had eaten a long lunch together down in the restaurant, and he'd even noticed a change in how his father treated the employees. He joked and laughed with them and assured them he was taking care of his health.

Even though his father had been in great shape —he played tennis and looked healthy enough— his doctor wanted him to start eating healthier, so he ordered a cob salad instead of his normal steak or cheeseburger. Luke had joined him, realizing that he too could use a lighter menu.

Over next few days, he kept waiting for his father's old side to show up. When they drove down to the Boardwalk Bar & Grill for dinner one night to meet Cassey, he was especially concerned his old ways would resurface.

The place was almost empty when they walked in. Cassey was talking to a few customers around the bar area. He still couldn't get over the fact that they were engaged. Every night when he'd talked to her, he'd wished he could be there to hold her.

When she smiled at them from across the room, his father whispered, "You hooked a good one."

He couldn't help but smile back.

Cassey was nervous. Even though she'd met Luke's father on several occasions, this time mattered the most, somehow. Luke had been telling her how his father had changed, but she still had to see it herself before she believed it.

She'd changed outfits three times before settling on a simple black and silver dress. The pearl choker and dangling pearl drops at her ears were simple yet elegant.

She couldn't believe she was thinking about

settling down, something she told herself she'd never do. She'd never held a relationship longer than a few weeks, and now she was planning on getting married after dating Luke for only four months.

Were they rushing it? she asked herself as she walked across the room to meet Luke's family. But when he smiled, all doubt left her mind, and she knew there was no way she wanted to live without him. He was everything she'd ever dreamed of finding.

"Evening." She watched as Luke walked towards her with his parents.

"Oh, isn't this place nice," Sophia said, looking around.

Cassey felt the need to apologize for the place being almost empty at six on a Thursday. She looked over at Luke's dad and held her tongue.

"You have a real nice place here," he said, shaking her hand firmly. Then he pulled closer and whispered. "And I'll do everything in my power to make sure it stays yours. You're family now." He pulled back and winked at her and she felt her heart skip.

The surprise must have shown on her face, because Luke pulled her closer and held onto her hand. When they walked over to their favorite booth, Luke whispered, "Crazy, huh?"

All she could do was nod.

"So, what do you suggest we have?" Jeffery asked, peeking over his menu.

"The Mahi Mahi po'boy is the best around," she suggested. "But I hear you're on a strict diet." She smiled. "The grilled shrimp salad is one of my favorites."

He chuckled. "I fear the days of eating what I want are long gone, but the salad sounds wonderful." He set his menu down.

Cassey noticed Sophia was smiling at her husband. "I think I'll have one of those as well."

When the food came, Luke's dad smiled. "Wow, this actually looks great. Here I was thinking it would be some leaves with grilled shrimp on top."

Cassey looked down at her salad and smiled. Sam had really outdone himself when he'd created this dish. The skewer of grilled shrimp was seasoned to perfection and sat on a plate of fresh lettuce, grilled red and green peppers, and slices of tomatoes, cucumbers, and pineapples. The seasoning and homemade zesty pineapple dressing were one of the reasons Cassey loved the dish so much.

After the meal, Luke's parents couldn't stop talking about how great the food was, so she walked them back to the kitchen and introduced them to Sam and the staff.

Luke's parents shook their hands and his father talked to Sam about some alternative healthy dishes.

After leaving the kitchen, Cassey suggested they walk along the boardwalk. She talked about her neighbors and the wonderful businesses along the beach.

"Some of these businesses have been here as long as I can remember," she said.

"I remember the arcade place when we were in school. It used to have bumper cars and a roller skating ring," Sophia said, reaching over and taking her husband's arm. Then she sighed. "Oh, the fun we had back then."

As they walked along, Cassey noticed a few of the empty buildings. It was hard for her to see them, knowing that Luke's father had had a hand in making them empty. But when they made it to the other end of the boardwalk, Luke's father started talking about how he could help make the place boom again.

"You know, I talked to my buddy down at city hall, and we're all on board to have the shuttles start up again. It seems that without places like this to go to, bookings are down. Apparently people want this"—he motioned around—"and not just the beaches themselves." Then he turned to his son. "Son, I'd like to help out with the place you're building."

Luke looked at his father cautiously, so much so that his father laughed. "Off the books, I promise."

Luke nodded. "That would be great."

"You know," he said, leaning one of his feet on the rung of the wood railings and looking out at the cold empty beach, "one of the main reasons I wanted to build here was all the great memories we had as kids." He reached over and took his wife's hand. "There's a lot of happiness here."

"It should stay as it is," Cassey piped in, causing everyone to look back at her.

"Oh, I don't know about that," Luke's father said. "I think there could still be some improvements here and there."

"We don't need big hotels coming in and taking over."

Jeffery smiled. "I would agree with you now. A few days ago..." He shook his head. "I suppose it's like everything else in my life. I wasn't seeing how great things were, even if they were right in front of my face." He winked at Luke and Cassey could see tears in his eyes.

His parents decided to go for a stroll along the beach. It was nice seeing them walk hand in hand along the shore. Cassey and Luke headed in the opposite direction.

"I like your dad," she said after a while.

He laughed. "I never thought I'd be able to say the same thing." He turned to her and shook his head. "I don't know what happened to him in physical therapy, but whatever it was, it was a blessing."

"You know, I was having second thoughts," she said, wrapping her arms around his neck.

"Really? Because of my father?"

She nodded. "You know what I came from." When he nodded, she continued. "I didn't want to put myself into a situation where I had to live with any kind of abuse again."

He pulled her closer. "I would never allow it to go that far."

"I know, but I didn't want to be the reason for the rift between you and your family."

He shook his head. "The rift started long before you." He ran his hand down her cheek.

She smiled a little. "I like your *new* dad."

He chuckled. "So do I. I just hope he sticks around. But if he doesn't, I'll always be here." He pulled her up and placed his warm mouth on hers. She felt the heat of the kiss all the way to her toes and at that moment, she knew that this is where she'd always been destined to be.

Epilogue

Cassey stood on the crowded boardwalk and watched the grand opening of the remodeled building. Several of the old buildings were getting face-lifts, thanks to her brother's business. Marcus had stayed busy in the last ten months working on remodeling the boardwalk and overseeing Luke's hotel construction.

Looking up and down the boardwalk now, you would never know that just a few months ago it had been on the verge of closing. She felt a hand in hers and looked over towards Luke.

"The place looks good, huh?"

She smiled. "Who would have thought that a little paint and some new windows would make such a big difference." She laughed when Luke's dad tried to cut the ribbon and it wouldn't break.

"If you had asked me a year ago if I believed my father would help me open an ice cream parlor, I would have laughed at you."

Actually, his father had helped finance three businesses along the boardwalk, thanks to the persistence of Luke and his mother.

"He looks good." She nodded towards his dad. "Happy and healthy."

He nodded. "The doctor says he's on the path to making a full recovery. He's the happiest I've ever seen him."

She sighed and leaned back against his shoulder. "He sure has changed a lot." Cassey knew that Luke's dad had cut back his work hours at Crystal Shores and was spending more time playing golf and tennis with his wife. They had even gone on two vacations in the last year and had taken Luke and her along to Maui just last month.

When she looked up and down the boardwalk, she saw booming businesses packed with tourists. Her place was back to its full potential thanks to Luke and his father's new business plans and the return of the shuttles.

"Next week we'll cut the ribbon on Surf Breeze Resorts." She turned in his arms and smiled. "Are you nervous?"

He chuckled and kissed her nose. "Not as nervous as I am about getting married the month after."

She tilted her head. "We could always postpone."

He shook his head and smiled. "Not a chance. If it was up to me, we would have been married a year ago."

She laughed and looked up into his dark eyes. "Yes, so you've told me."

They stood on the boardwalk, holding each other as they looked around. Friends, family, and strangers were crowded onto the old boards enjoying the sun as the waves hit the white sands of the beaches.

She'd come a long way from the little girl who had been found hiding in the forest. She'd never really allowed herself to trust someone as much as she trusted Luke now. He'd proven to her that he would do anything, including giving up his family, to ensure that she was happy. She'd never experienced that kind of love before, nor had she ever dreamed she'd love someone that much in return.

"What do you say to letting me buy you some ice cream?" Luke asked.

"I'd love some." She smiled as he took her hand and they started walking down the boardwalk, together.

Jill Sanders

Loving Lauren - Preview
Prologue

Hot wind whirled around Lauren's skirt, causing it to fly up. She laughed as she twirled around. Stopping for a second to catch her breath, she looked over at her sisters, Alex and Haley. Alex's bright blonde head was pointed downward as she sat in the dirt, happily making a mud pile. Haley's dark curly hair lay in the grass as she watched the clouds rush by.

Lauren looked up at the sky and noticed that the clouds were going by very fast. Frowning a little, she decided that dancing some more while keeping her eyes glued to the sky might be fun. She twirled while watching everything rush by her, almost causing her to tumble over and fall.

Dancing in the fields was one of her greatest joys. Even though she had to babysit her younger sisters today, she didn't mind. For the most part, her sisters could entertain themselves. Lauren still had to carry Haley sometimes when her short legs got tired. She supposed that being four was tiring, though she couldn't remember ever being four. She thought she must have slept through her life until she turned five, when her first memories happened. Haley was always asleep, or lying down, like now. But Lauren was eight and she had enough energy to shake the roof off the barn, or so her Daddy always said.

The breeze moved the tall grass around them, making the field look as if it were dancing with her. She stopped to bow to her make-believe dance partner, a move she'd seen late one night when she had sneaked to the edge of the stairs. Her parents had been watching an old black-and-white movie and she could make out the screen if she tilted her head just right. The woman in the long white dress had bowed slowly while smiling at a tall gentlemen in a black suit and tie. They'd looked so wonderful. From that moment on, Lauren had wanted to dance. Every chance she had, she'd moved around like she'd watched the couple do, wishing her dress was longer so it would flow like the lady's had.

Taking a break, she looked off towards the house. The large three-story stone place sat like a beacon in the yellow fields. Its bright white pillars gleamed in the sunlight, at least when the clouds weren't shadowing the land. It was the only place she'd ever known as home. Her dad's dad had built the place a long, long time ago. Probably a zillion years ago. The outside looked new, and her dad did everything he could to keep the inside looking new, too. But Lauren knew some of the floorboards creaked when you walked on them. And the water only stayed hot long enough for her and her sisters to share a bath at night. But worst of all, she had blue carpet in her bedroom. Lauren hated blue. She'd begged her dad for new carpet, yellow preferably. Her dad told her it was blue because it used to be his room, and that it would have to stay blue until they could afford new carpet. Her room was perfect, except for the blue carpet. It was like a big wart on her room. Not that she'd ever gotten warts. Jenny Steven's had a wart once on her finger and she had to wear a My Little Pony Band-Aid over it. But during recess, Jenny had pulled the Band-Aid off and shown Lauren her wart. It was gross, all wet and puffy. So Lauren thought of her blue carpet as a wart on the face of her bedroom.

Looking at the house, she knew her mama was back in the kitchen making a feast for the church potluck tomorrow. Everyone was going to be there, even Dale Bennett. She didn't like Dale; he always pulled her hair and pushed her into the dirt, even when she was wearing her new church dress.

She knew that her mama was the best cook in the county. Or so her daddy always said.

Hearing a loud noise, she looked off towards the dark clouds that were forming over the hills. Her daddy was somewhere up in the hills, gathering the cows. She didn't know why they had to move the cows around all the time. It was still a mystery to her why they couldn't just stay here in the fields. There was plenty of tall grass to eat right here, close to the house. Another loud sound came from the hills. At first, Lauren thought it was a gunshot. She'd heard a lot of those growing up on the huge ranch, but then she turned her head a little and heard her mother screaming for them.

"Girls! Run, come quick!" Her mother stood in the front door, her apron flowing in the wind as her hands motioned for them to come to her.

"Come on. Mama wants us to run," Lauren told her sisters.

Alex stood and dusted off her hands and started skipping towards the house. Haley on the other hand didn't move.

"Come on, Haley, Mama wants us to run home." Another loud noise came from behind her and when she looked, the sky had turned black. Fear shot through her like a bolt of lightning. Without saying a word, Lauren grabbed up her baby sister and started running. Since her legs were longer than Alexis', she made it to her skipping sister and screamed for her to run faster. Halfway to the house, Lauren had to set Haley down. Her little sister had gained a few pounds and was too heavy for her to carry the entire way. Their mother wasn't in the doorway when they got there; instead, she was standing in the hallway.

"Quick, we have to get to the shelter." Her mother picked up Haley and started running towards the back door.

"Mama, Bear!" Haley screamed. "I want Bear!"

Their old deaf dog was lying by the fireplace, where he always stayed, taking a nap.

"Fine." Their mother set Haley down next to her and looked Lauren in the eyes. At this time, Lauren could hear the wind rushing through the house. The sound was so loud that Haley covered her ears and started to cry. "Lauren, I want you to make sure you get your sisters into the shelter, like I taught you. Can you do that?"

Lauren remembered the drills Mama and Papa had put her through. Nodding her head, she grabbed her sisters' hands. "Yes, Mama."

"Good. Now run," her mother yelled over the noise, then she took off down the hallway to grab the dog as Lauren turned and started running, dragging her sisters behind her. When they got to the kitchen, Alex stopped. She pulled her hand out of Lauren's and started grabbing cookies that their mother had been baking.

"No, Alex, we have to go now." Lauren dropped Haley's hand and grabbed Alex by the shoulders, causing her to drop all the cookies.

"No, I'm gonna tell Mama." Alex started crying. Here in the back of the house the noise was even louder. She could see grass and leaves fly by the windows when she looked out.

"We have to get to the shelter, or Mama is going tell Daddy." That stopped her sister from picking up the dropped cookies. Lauren grabbed her hand and turned back to get Haley, but Haley was gone. Just then their mother came into the kitchen carrying the old dog.

"Where's Haley?" she screamed, as she held the old dog in her arms.

"I don't know. She was just here. Then Alex—"

"Here, we don't have time for stories now. Take Bear and Alex and get to the shelter. Run girls, run!" Her mother pushed Bear into her arms. The dog looked small in her mother's arms, but in hers, he was heavy. She had to shift his fat body to make sure she didn't drop him. Alex ran to the back door and opened it. Hearing her mother's urgent tone, she must have understood that something bad was happening.

The girls rushed across the backyard through the high wind and the heavy rain that was falling. When they reached the storm shelter, Lauren had to set Bear down to open the big door. Alex grabbed Bear's collar, making sure he didn't run away as Lauren pushed the door open. Then Alex pulled Bear down the stairs as Lauren looked back towards the house. She could see a light go on in her sister's bedroom, then her mother's shadow crossed the window. Her mother bent down, and when she stood back up, Lauren could see that Haley was in her arms. She felt relieved until she looked up.

"Run, Mama!" Lauren screamed. The dark clouds circled above the house, and Lauren's little body froze to the spot outside the shelter. It seemed like hours later when her mother finally appeared at the back door holding Haley. Her sister's head was buried in her mother's apron.

"Get inside!" her mother screamed halfway across the backyard.

Lauren's feet became unglued and she rushed to the bottom of the stairs. Turning, she waited for her mother to reach the shelter door. She watched as her mother's dress flew sideways in the high winds. Haley was holding onto her apron tightly.

Then everything slowed down in Lauren's mind. Her mother, a few steps from the doorway, looked up quickly, then turned her head and looked right at her. Lifting Haley high, she threw her into the open doorway. Haley fell down the stairs, and her little body hit Lauren's with enough force that it knocked them down. Haley's body shook as she cried, still clutching a piece of their mother's apron, which had been ripped from her shoulders. Lauren quickly got up and stood on the floor of the shelter, looking up into the doorway. She watched in terror as the ferocious winds ripped her mother from the doorway and swept her into the darkness.

Jill Sanders

Chapter One

Ten years later...

Lauren looked down at the grave as a tear slipped down her nose. It was a week before her nineteenth birthday, and she watched as her father's closest friends lowered his casket into the ground. She heard her sisters crying beside her and blindly reached over and took both of their hands. It had been two days since she'd found her father lying on his bedroom floor. She'd done everything she'd known to try and save him, but she'd been too late. She'd do anything to go back and somehow get to the house earlier that sunny day.

Closing her eyes, she could remember her father's face, his kindness, the way he moved and smelled, and the way he talked. Everything about the man had told his daughter's that he loved them, that he'd do anything for them. They'd lost their mother ten years ago; their father had picked up the pieces and raised three girls on his own. They had all missed their mother, but thanks to their father, they had grown up knowing that they were loved. They had never gone to bed hungry, dirty, or without a bedtime story.

If the food had been a little burnt or a little odd tasting, the girls never complained. Even when Alex's costume for the school play had turned out looking more like a green leaf than a tree, she hadn't complained. When Lauren had finally hit the age to legally drive, she'd taken it upon herself to drive her sisters to and from school and any other after school functions they'd been involved in, even if it meant forgoing her own social life.

The guilt had always played in the back of her mind. *If I had just watched Haley better. If I had just kept holding her hand, Mama would be here today.*

The school had offered the girls counseling, but Lauren had just sat through it and had told the older woman who had been assigned to counsel her what she'd wanted to hear. Not once did she hint that it was her fault that their mother was gone. Not once did she confide in anyone that she was to blame.

When her father was in the ground, she closed her eyes and lifted her face to the sky. The spring Texas air felt wonderful. She knew that in a little over a month, the breeze would be hot enough to steam the tears that were falling down her face. The cool wind would stop and be replaced by stillness and heat. But for now, she enjoyed the smell of the grass growing, the flowers blooming, and the sight of the cherry trees that were planted around the small cemetery. Her father had always loved the spring. He'd been looking forward to helping her plant a new flower garden near the back of the house.

Now who was she going to plant flowers with? She opened her eyes and looked at Alexis. Her blonde hair was tied up in a simple bun at the base of her neck. Her black skirt and gray shirt were in complete contrast to her sister's normal attire. Even though Alex had just turned sixteen, her wild side had been on the loose for the last two years. So much so that it had started eating up a lot of Lauren's and their father's time.

"Your sister is going to be the death of me. Mark my words, Lauren. Someday you're going to walk in and she'll be standing over my cold body, complaining about the fact that she can't have a pair of hundred-dollar jeans."

In fact, Alex hadn't been home that day. She'd stayed the night at a friend's house that entire weekend.

Lauren looked over at Haley. She was too young to remember their mother. And even though they'd never talked about it, she knew her sister was a little jealous of the fact that Lauren and Alex could both remembered her.

As the minister, a longtime family friend, was saying his closing, Lauren looked down at her father's final resting place. What was she going to do now? How were they going to live without him?

Her shoulders sank a little as she walked forward and tossed a white rose into the hole, onto her father's casket. When she turned and stepped away, she looked off to the distance. West of here was Saddleback Ranch, their home for as long as she could remember. It had been handed down for three generations now.

Straightening her shoulders and looking off to the distance, she knew in her heart that she'd do anything—anything—to keep it. To keep her and her sisters together. On their land. Like her father and mother would have wanted her to do.

After shaking the hands of and hugging almost everyone in the small three-thousand-person strong community, she stood outside her truck talking briefly with Grant Holton Sr., her father's lawyer and one of his best friends. Mr. Holton was tall and very broad chested. She'd heard once that he and her father had played football together.

She looked over as Dr. Graham and his son, Chase, walked up to them. Dr. Graham had been the ranch's veterinarian. Every animal on her land was healthy thanks to the older man who walked forward and shook her hand with a firm grip. Chase had been a year ahead of her in school. They'd grown up together and had even gone to a couple dances together in high school and had shared a few stolen kisses behind the bleachers. But then he'd graduated and she'd seen less and less of him.

Chase was tall like his father. It looked like he'd tried to grease back his bushy mass of black hair for the ceremony. She'd always loved pushing her hands into his thick hair. His dark brown eyes stared at her with sincere concern and grief, much like his father's did now.

"Lauren." Dr. Graham shook her hand, then Mr. Holton's.

Mr. Holton nodded, then turned towards her. "I know this isn't the time to think about your future or the ranch's future, but maybe we can meet tomorrow. Just the three of us. There are a few details I need to go over with you."

At that moment, realization hit her—she was the head of the house. She was now in charge of a thousand-acre ranch. In charge of her sisters. In charge of the cattle, the horses, everything. She must have paled a little, because Chase stepped forward and took her elbow. "Are you okay?" he whispered.

She wanted to shove his arm away and scream. "No! I'm not okay, you idiot. Everything is ruined! I have no family left." But instead, she nodded and swayed a little, causing him to move his other arm around her waist. "Dad," Chase said, looking towards his father.

"Quite right, we apologize." The older man cleared his throat, looking towards his friend.

"No," Lauren blinked. If she wanted to keep the three of them on her family's land, she would just have to step up a little more. Remember, she told herself, keep your sisters together and do whatever it takes to stay on your family's land. "If you want, I'm heading back to the house now. We can meet in say"—she looked at her watch as Chase dropped his arm—"an hour?"

Dr. Graham and Mr. Holton nodded their heads in unison. She could see the questions in their eyes. Lauren turned when she spotted her sisters walking towards her. She walked stiffly around to the driver's side of her truck, her shoulders square. As they drove away in silence, she looked back and saw the three men standing there. A shiver rolled down her back and she knew at that moment that everything was going to change.

The drive to the ranch wasn't a long one. It sat almost ten miles outside of town, but the roads were always empty and the highway stretched in a straight line. When they passed the old iron gate with Saddleback Ranch overhead, she felt a little peace settle in her bones. There, in the distance, stood the three-story house she'd always known and loved. It had taken some bangs in its time. The tornado that had claimed their mother had torn the roof right off the massive place. The old red barn had been flattened back then as well. They'd lost a dozen horses and two of the farmhand houses. Thank goodness her father and the men had been in the hills that day, or they might have been caught up in the storm as well. But the barn and farmhands' houses had been rebuilt. The house had gotten a shiny new roof, along with a new paint job and some new windows panes to replace the ones that had blown out. After her father replaced the storm cellar's door, no one talked about that day anymore.

Lauren stopped the truck in front of the barn, and Haley jumped out and ran through the massive doors. Alex turned and looked at Lauren.

"Don't worry. I'll go talk to her." Lauren patted her sister's thigh and got out of the truck. Dingo, the family dog, an Australian shepherd mix, rushed up to Lauren and jumped on her dress. "No, down." She pushed the dog off, but she followed her into the dark barn.

Outside, the sun had warmed her, but here in the darkness of the barn, the coolness seeped into her bones. She rubbed her arms with her hands as she walked forward to climb the old stairs that led to the second floor, where she knew her sister would be.

The loft was huge, taking up three quarters of the barn, but Lauren knew Haley's hiding places and walked right to her sister. Haley was stretched out on the soft hay, her best Sunday dress fanned out around her. She was face down and crying like there was no tomorrow. Lauren walked over and sat next to her. She pulled her into her arms and cried with her.

Less than an hour later, Lauren had changed into her work clothes and stood at the door to greet Mr. Holton, Dr. Graham, and, to her surprise, Chase. The four of them walked into her father's large office and she shut the glass doors behind her. Taking a large breath, she turned to face the room.

"Please, have a seat." She motioned for the three men to sit as she walked around her father's massive desk and sat in his soft leather chair. She'd done it a hundred times, but this time it felt different.

"Your father was a great man," Mr. Holton started. "He was our best friend." He looked at Dr. Graham, and the other man nodded his head in agreement. "We could postpone this meeting for —"

"No, please." Lauren straightened her shoulders.

"Very well." Mr. Holton pulled out a file from his briefcase. "As you know, I am your father's lawyer. John, here"—he nodded to Dr. Graham —"well, he has a stake in what we need to discuss. That's why I invited him along."

"Continue," Lauren said when she thought Mr.

Holton had lost his nerve. She knew it was bad news; she could see it clearly on both man's faces.

"Well, after that day"—Mr. Holton cleared his throat and shifted in his seat—"after we lost your mother, Richard took out some loans."

"Mr. Holton, how much did my father owe the bank?" She wanted the bottom line. Holding her breath, she waited.

"Well, that's the tricky part. You see, Richard didn't trust in banks all that much." The two older men looked between themselves. "Maybe this will explain it better." He set the file on the desk in front of her.

She opened the file with shaky fingers. There, in her father's handwriting, was her future.

I, Richard West, being of sound body and mind, do solemnly promise to pay back the total sum of $100,000.00 to Johnathan Graham Sr. and Grant Holton II. If anything should happen to me, the proceeds of my ranch, Saddleback Ranch, would go to both men in equal amounts until paid back in full. They would have a say in the running of the ranch until said amount was paid in full.

It had been dated and signed by her father, John Graham, and Grant Holton Sr. over ten years ago.

"I understand your concerns." She looked up from the paper. "As head of the house now, I will fulfill my father's obligations."

"Well, that's all well and good." Dr. Graham

smiled. "But, well, we had an understanding between the three of us. If anything happened to him and we saw that you three or the ranch was in any jeopardy, we'd step in and run this place until we saw fit."

Lauren listened as the men told her the scheme the three of them—her father, Mr. Holton and Dr. Graham—had come up with ten years ago in case anything like this should happen. How they'd take over the running of the land, the handling of the finances, even deciding how to deal with her and her sisters. She was being pushed out before she'd even had the chance to try and run things her way. She'd practically raised her sisters, and now these two men wanted to take control of everything, even her. Her heart sank upon hearing this news. She asked for some time to think about it and the men apologized and quickly excused themselves.

After the older men had driven away, Chase stayed behind and offered her another option. The next day Lauren stood in front of the courthouse in Tyler, wearing her Sunday best. She knew her life would never be the same again after that day.

Seven years later...

Chase stood in the middle of the street and took

a deep breath. He was finally home. It wasn't that he'd been avoiding the place, or that he hadn't had the will to return, but life had led him down a twisted path. He was happy that he'd finally ended up back here, at least for now. A car horn honked at him, and he waved and moved from the center of the road. Walking up the stone steps to his father's building, he realized that the old green place had never looked better. He knew the money he'd been sending home over the last nine years had helped with fixing up the clinic.

When he opened the front door, the bell above the door chimed and he smiled.

"Morning, how can I—" Cheryl, his father's receptionist, stood slowly. "Son of a..."

"Now, Cheryl, you know you're not supposed to say that around here." He walked forward and received her welcome hug. The woman almost engulfed him, but he smiled and took the beating as she patted his back hard. Her arms were like vices, but her front was soft and she smelled just like he remembered, like chocolate and wet puppies. The odd mix of aromas had always warmed his spirits.

"What are you doing back in town?" she asked. She gasped. "Does your father know?" She looked toward the back room.

He shook his head. "I wanted to surprise him." He smiled.

Her smile slipped a little. "Well, you sure will." Then she bit her bottom lip and he knew something was up.

"Spill." He took her shoulders before she could turn away.

"What?" She tried to look innocent.

"Cheryl, how long have I known you?"

She smiled. "Going on twenty-eight years next June." He smiled. Cheryl always did remembered his birthday.

"And in all that time, I've come to know that when you bite your bottom lip, you have something you're trying to hide. So..."—he motioned with his hand—"spill."

She crossed her arms over her chest. "Fine. It's just your father's health. I know he hasn't mentioned it over the phone to you."

"What about it?" Chase began to get worried and felt like rushing to the back room to check up on his dad. Cheryl had never mentioned anything personal about his father's health in their conversations. Neither had his father.

"Well, he injured his leg a while back." She twisted her shirtfront.

"And?" He waited.

"And, well, he's walking with a cane now," she blurted out, just as his father walked through the back door.

"Thank you, Cheryl. That will be enough out of you." His father smiled. Sure enough, his father was leaning on a black cane. "Well, boy?" He held out his arm. "Don't make me hobble over to you for that hug."

Chase rushed across the room and gave his old man a bear hug like he always had, noticing that his father was not only skinnier, but felt frailer. He had a million questions he wanted to ask, but knew his father wouldn't answer until he was good and ready.

"Come on back here, boy. Tell me what you've been up to." His father started walking towards the back and Chase watched him hobble. Then his father turned. "Are you back to stay?"

"Yes," Chase said absentmindedly. He hadn't meant to stay, had he?

"Good." His father turned into his office and took a seat, setting the cane down beside him. Chase sat in the chair across from him, waiting.

"Well, I suppose I should tell you, you couldn't have come home at a better time. I'm retiring."

"What?" Chase sat up. His father raised his hands, holding off the million questions he had.

"Yes, at the end of the year. I've been kicked one too many times." His father smiled. "This old body doesn't want to work like it used to. I was going to give you a call later this month."

"Dad?" He looked at him.

287

"I know, I know. I told you I'd never retire, but..." he looked down at his leg. "The doctors are telling me I have to be off this damned leg for six hours a day. Six! You and I both know that in this line of work you'd be lucky to sit for five minutes a day."

Chase smiled. "I guess it's a good thing I'm home, then."

His father smiled and nodded his head. "What do you say we go grab some lunch? I'm buying."

Fairplay, Texas, had one place to sit and eat. Mama's Diner, a huge brown barn that had been turned into a restaurant, had been the best place to eat in two counties since as far back as Chase could remember. Even now the place looked new and smelled like greasy burgers.

His father took his usual booth. It almost made Chase laugh, knowing the man never sat in a different spot. Even if someone was in it, he'd stand and wait until the table was cleared. There were new menus and he took his time looking over the list of new items.

"How are you today, beautiful?" his father asked the waitress when she stopped by.

Chase looked up and stared into the most beautiful green eyes he'd ever seen. Her hair was longer than before, and her dark curls hung just below the most perfect breasts he'd ever had the pleasure of being up against. She was tall and limber and he could remember the softness of

288

every curve he'd been allowed to feel. She looked down at him like he was in her way and he started coughing. He couldn't explain how it happened, but he was choking on air. Nothing was getting through to his lungs or to his brain. Finally, she smacked his back hard, and he took a deep breath. He stood and grabbed Lauren's arm and demanded in a low voice, "What the hell are you doing working here?"

Other books by Jill Sanders

The Pride Series
Finding Pride – Pride Series #1
Discovering Pride – Pride Series #2
Returning Pride – Pride Series #3
Lasting Pride – Pride Series #4
Serving Pride – Prequel to Pride Series #5
Red Hot Christmas – A Pride Christmas #6
My Sweet Valentine – Pride Series #7
Summer Crush – Pride Series #8

The Secret Series
Secret Seduction – Secret Series #1
Secret Pleasure – Secret Series #2
Secret Guardian – Secret Series #3
Secret Passions – Secret Series #4
Secret Identity – Secret Series #5
Secret Sauce – Secret Series #6

The West Series
Loving Lauren – West Series #1
Taming Alex – West Series #2
Holding Haley – West Series #3
Missy's Moment – West Series #4
Breaking Travis - West Series #5
Roping Ryan - West Series #6
Wild Bride – West Series #7

The Grayton Series
Last Resort – Book #1

For a complete list of books, visit JillSanders.com

This is a work of fiction. Names, characters, places, and incidents are either the product of the author's imagination or are used fictitiously, and any resemblance to actual persons, living or dead, business establishments, events, or locales is entirely coincidental.

PRINT ISBN: 978-1507663233
DIGITAL ISBN: 978-1-942896-00-5
Copyright © 2014 Jill Sanders
Copyeditor: Erica Ellis – inkdeepediting.com

About the Author

Jill Sanders is the New York Times and USA Today bestselling author of the Pride Series, Secret Series and West Series romance novels. Having sold over 150,000 books within 6 months of her first release, she continues to lure new readers with her sweet and sexy stories. Her books are available in every English speaking country and are now being translated to 6 different languages, and recorded for audiobook.

Born as an identical twin in a large family, she was raised in the Pacific Northwest. She later relocated to Colorado for college and a successful IT career before discovering her talent as a writer. She now makes her home in charming rural Florida where she enjoys the beach, swimming, hiking, wine tasting, and, of course, writing.

50773745R00164

Made in the USA
San Bernardino, CA
03 July 2017